CIRCLE OF WATER

THE WITCH'S PROGRESS
BOOK THREE

LEAH R CUTTER

KNOTTED ROAD PRESS

Come someplace new…
Are you a traveler? Do you enjoy exploring strange new worlds, new cultures, new people?

Journey into the various lands envisioned by Leah Cutter.

Sign up for my newsletter and I'll start you on your travels with a free copy of my book, *The Island Sampler*.

I will never spam you or use your email for nefarious purposes. You can also unsubscribe at any time.

http://www.LeahCutter.com/newsletter/

The Ghost Dog

The Shadow Wars Trilogy

The Raven and the Dancing Tiger

The Guardian Hound

War Among the Crocodiles

The Clockwork Fairy Kingdom

The Clockwork Fairy Kingdom

The Maker, the Teacher, and the Monster

The Dwarven Wars

The Chronicles of Franklin

Franklin Versus The Popcorn Thief

Franklin Versus The Soul Thief

Franklin Versus The Child Thief

Contemporary Fantasy

Siren's Call

The Immortals' War

THE CIRCLES OF WITCHCRAFT

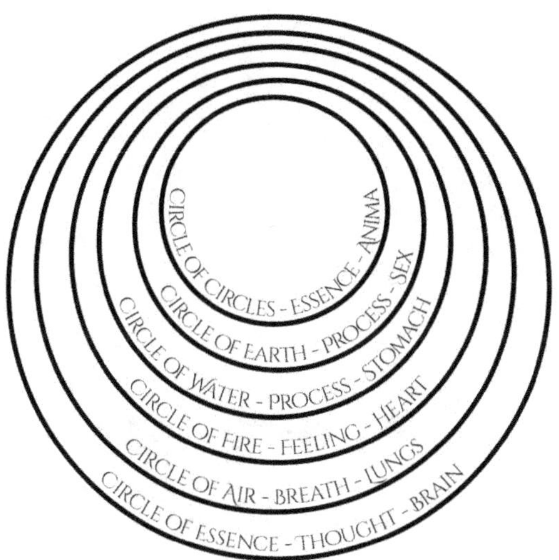

CHAPTER 1

Horrible flooding continues to plague Portland, the jewel of the Pacific Northwest. The mighty river god Mulinohana spares the bridges that I have marked as sacred. But He only spares those structures. The inhabitants of this city do not help their case, spewing filth and refuse into the clean waters. They are starting to be aware of their predicament, how they poison their own nests, and are planning to build what they're calling a seawall. Part of the work will divert the sewers from pouring into the river. While Mulinohana would be pleased with that, the wall itself displeases Him, as does anything that impedes His mighty flow. I will need to mark the wall as sacred, though I do not believe that a witch's heart placed at the base of the wall will be adequate. It is not a single base, unlike a bridge. I will need to find something else to

sacrifice so that the seawall can be built and the city will have more protection from the ever capricious river.

Wilson Evermore, Civil Engineer and Protector of Portland, 1920

WHEN TARA SAT UP IN HER BED, SHE SAW YET ANOTHER plain envelope had been slipped under the door to her room during the night. It wasn't addressed to her, but she knew it was meant for her, as all the others had been.

Though Tara loved her room in the house that she shared with four other people, the notes left her feeling uneasy. The smell of wet sisal rope washed through the air instead of the usual comforting scents of coffee and toast. She couldn't hear any of her roommates—they were either still asleep (like Tobias, who worked in a band) or already gone to work.

With a sigh, Tara pushed herself out of her bed, grabbing the ratty, dark green bathrobe that hung on the bedpost and wrapping herself in that. It enveloped her in a warm, soft hug. She sat down on the floor gracefully, thankful once again for the yoga classes that kept her limber even as she approached her thirties, tucking her straight brown hair behind her ears.

The envelope was manila colored and the size that would normally contain a happy greeting card. This one, like the others, contained a newspaper clipping from the day before, pasted to a white sheet of paper. The news reported two boats crashing into each other. One woman had been killed and three men hospitalized.

In block letters on the white paper was printed,

"YOUR FAULT." The words looked as though they'd been drawn in red crayon. At least the words felt waxy, and she didn't think they were done in blood.

Tara shook her head. How could a stupid drunken boating accident be her fault? Yet, every time there was an accident on the river or a body was dredged out of the waters, someone—probably the Riprap man—sent her a clipping like this. It had been going on for the last six months.

It wasn't as if there hadn't been accidents when he'd still been bonded to the river spirit Mulinohana. Now that the water spirit was free, it wasn't suddenly causing a bunch of deaths, no matter what the Riprap man might think.

Though there had been more bodies found floating in the river during the last six months. Most of the cases were labeled as suicide or accidental drowning—there were very few homicides. For the previous two years, a body was found floating in the Willamette river about once every ten days, which was considerably more than any other city. Over the last two months, that number had increased to about one per week.

It wasn't her fault. Or at least she kept telling herself that.

Still, the envelope and the clipping were always distressing. Tara put the paper back down on the floor, her hands shaking.

Suddenly, a warm presence pressed against her right side. Tara knew without looking that Soot had just shown up, the tamed wind who took the appearance of a black greyhound. She put her arm over his shoulders and rested her head against him, letting his warmth comfort her.

Not to be left out, Tara heard a loud "Mrrr," and felt a head butting her left leg. She reached out to pet Teruko, the tamed fire spirit who looked like a calico cat, primarily white with brown and black patches, as well as a short, stubby tail. Teruko promptly stepped up onto Tara's thigh, then dropped down into her lap, purring hard. She, too, had come to comfort Tara.

One of the reasons why Tara had chosen this house was because her housemates let her have pets, though they frequently remarked on how quiet her animals were, as well as how they seemed to get in and out of the house on their own, without using a door.

Teruko turned her head up to Tara and issued another "Mrr"?

Tara looked down into the kitty's eyes, one pale blue, the other golden brown. She wasn't sure if Teruko wanted more pets or was asking what to do next.

Or maybe both, as she immediately head-butted Tara's hand when it got in reach.

"I don't know what we're going to do," Tara told her two familiars. Only hedgewitches had familiars and could tame elements. Schooled witches didn't keep them.

Then again, Tara would call Soot and Teruko merely half tamed. They would only do her bidding about half of the time. Otherwise, they ignored her, walked away, and went along on their own business. Ginny, the other hedgewitch in Tara's coven, told her this was normal.

It made someone like Tara, who tended to be logical and organized, quite crazy sometimes. But she was trying to be more spontaneous. At least during her off hours.

Tara shook her head. "I have to get going, you

two," she said after a few more skritches to both spirits. "Teaching this morning, volunteering this afternoon."

Teruko looked up at that. "Mrrr?" she asked.

Tara thought for a moment. "Yes, you can come," she said. While both spirits tended to follow her wherever she went, whether she wanted them around or not, they respected Hallowed Ground, the homeless shelter where Tara volunteered. It was Kaede's space. While Teruko and Soot could push their way through Kaede's protection spells, they both were happier when they didn't have to, when Tara granted them permission to come with her.

That afternoon, Tara was running the "teashop" in the homeless shelter. Having Teruko with her would be good. The cat would sit on one corner of the countertop, happy for people to pet her while Tara made up their order. It frequently allowed Tara to talk longer with the person, listening and asking questions, so that she could learn what the person really needed, not just what they'd asked for.

Soot helped too, playing with the younger children. He acted like a puppy around them, though the rest of the time he seemed like a mature dog.

"Okay, so let me get up and get going," Tara told her companions. With a sigh, Teruko got up on all fours, stretched her back, then languidly stepped first, onto Tara's thigh, then onto the floor. Soot snuffled her hair, rubbing his cold nose behind her ear, before he also stepped away.

Tara stood up easily, stretching her arms up above her head, then from side to side. It would be a long day today; however, she also knew that it would be satisfying. Nothing she did ever felt like work anymore. It was a strange place to be.

First, though, as she'd promised, she sent a mass email to everyone in her coven, letting them know that she'd received yet another missive from the Riprap man. She didn't have to face this on her own, though it was still difficult for her to ask for help. And it wasn't as if the Riprap man had challenged her.

The winter solstice had come and gone without incident. While Tara had had nightmares, they were of her own making, not dreams sent to her.

With a start, Tara realized that the spring equinox was only a week away. It was Thursday, and the equinox was the following Wednesday night.

Would the Riprap man try something then? Or was she still safe?

She included that tidbit in the email before she sent it off, then went to prepare for the long day ahead.

TARA WALKED UP THE STREET, HEADING FOR HALLOWED Ground. Her hair was still wet from her shower earlier, rinsing off all the chlorine from the pool. She'd spent several hours teaching that day—seniors' water aerobics, beginning swimming for toddlers, as well as coaching a half dozen men who'd made an arrangement with the Y and were getting tips for their coming triathlon.

The building itself looked like an older office building, built in the 1920s. It originally would have had retail on the ground floor and goods displayed in the big picture windows on either side of the door in the center of the building, with three floors above it full of apartments. Now, the ground floor was a dedicated community space and soup kitchen, and the upstairs rooms were given to the homeless who were truly in need.

Tara walked past the front door, down the alley on the side, and around to the back where the volunteers came and left.

Kaede, the person who ran the shelter, was a fifth level witch, and was very good with spaces. It was extremely difficult to permanently enchant an artifact. Most of the time, a sachet filled with herbs only lasted a few days, then would have to be replaced.

However, Hallowed Ground belonged to Kaede, and ze protected the entire building. Every time Tara walked in, she had the sensation of stepping into another place, a location that was separate from the mundane world, sacred, in a good way.

Big signs next to the door proclaimed that this entrance was for Volunteers Only—and that means YOU. The door was generally left unlocked, at least during the day. Because of the protections Kaede set in the building, very few people who weren't volunteers tried to come in that way.

Soot and Teruko appeared on either side of Tara as she opened the door. Though it was just an illusion that she was stepping into a dark, unwelcome hallway, it always gave her pause.

"Shall we?" Tara said as she stepped across the threshold. Her familiars walked in with her. Soot always gave himself a huge shake after he walked into the shelter, as if shedding the cold barrier from his fur.

Teruko did the same, stopping to give the fur on her back a few licks.

The small hallway was still dark, but it no longer felt foreboding. Kaede's office stood behind the first door to Tara's left. Only when Tara stopped and studied the door could she see the white chalk drawn on the white paint, promising pain to any who tried to enter without permission.

Kaede had never been forthcoming about where ze'd learned such a spell, or even where most of zir training had come from.

However, the spells on the door always reminded Tara of her first mentor, Miss Lucy, who didn't necessarily practice black magic, but tainted magic, nonetheless.

Past the office door, on the other side, lay a huge kitchen, at least thirty feet on a side, with a vaulted ceiling that rose up two stories. Though the florescent overhead lights were off, enough light to see by came in through the second story windows. Industrial ovens, stoves, and grills lined the walls, while a huge dishwasher/sanitizer stood in the corner. The air still smelled of the soap used to clean the linoleum floor. The room wasn't heated—the stoves were enough to keep the place warm when it was being used.

That afternoon, it was empty, everything put away. Instead of a permanent center island, the kitchen had a series of tables that volunteers put together as needed. Even those had been folded up and stood stacked against the far wall.

From the laughter that came from the main room at the end of the hall, Tara could tell that the after school program had already started. She wasn't late necessarily, but she would probably have a line waiting to talk with her as soon as she finished setting up.

A black curtain hung down over one of the long, industrial steel tables that had been pushed to the side, next to the dishwasher. That was Tara's space. When she reached for the curtain, the fabric scratched against her palms. Though this was *hers*, the spell on the curtain was so strong that it made even her feel uneasy.

A large collection of coffee containers full of herbs lay scattered across the lower shelf of the table. None of the containers were matched. They were the cheapest containers Tara could get at Goodwill. However, they all had good rubber seals on them, to prevent air from getting in.

Tara loaded all the containers onto a cart before flicking the curtain back down. She went looking for mugs next, but found the cupboard was empty.

Smiling, Tara wheeled her cart out into the main room. Long tables had been set up in three rows close to the hallway entrance, taking up just a small amount of space. A corner had been marked off for the younger kids to race around and play in. In another corner, an older member of the community—Stella, if Tara was remembering correctly—sat in a chair and read to a group of spellbound younger kids. Soot sat beside the storyteller, attentively listening with his tail thwapping.

One of the teens supposedly doing homework at the long table closest to the door came bounding up when he saw Tara—Eric. She'd made him a special tea the first time she'd volunteered at Hallowed Ground, and he'd become her determined helper ever since.

Eric looked better than when she'd first met him. He was still too skinny, with dirty blond hair that stuck up everywhere. But his gray-green eyes no longer looked so haunted, and his skin was no longer a washed-out white. He'd recently had a growing spurt, and was finally taller than Tara's five foot ten. He was just sixteen, and hadn't reached the end of his growth, she knew.

"I got out the mugs for you," Eric said as he helped her maneuver the cart next to the long table.

"Thank you," Tara said. The containers weren't marked, so Eric stood to the side, awkwardly shuffling from one foot to the other as Tara placed them in order. When she was finished putting the two dozen containers into three long rows, he cocked his head to one side and studied them.

"How did you order them this time?" he asked.

"What is your guess?" Tara replied.

He pressed his lips together and studied the arrangement. "The rose-colored short container has dried marigold flower petals. Adds brightness to a tea." He paused, then indicated the other end of the first line. "While hyssop flowers mellows out most teas, making them richer and darker."

"Very good!" Tara said. Eric had been fascinated by all the herbs she'd used, and had started learning the properties of each. He had no magic, at least as far as she could tell. He did, however, have a fantastic palate, and had been able to separate out the herbs of the "surprise" teas that she made for him.

She wanted to encourage him to get a job as a cook, and maybe train to be a chef. However, he was still too tightly wound to handle the stress of a kitchen. He would only meditate with her. Wouldn't do it on his own. Or at least not yet.

Eric helped Tara fill the giant jugs she used for water, then she filled her electric tea kettle and started the water boiling. She still envied the professional teashops and their massive hot water heaters that were able to keep the temperatures precise, based on the type of tea. Maybe some year, if she opened her own teashop, she could get some of those.

"Can I make you a tea?" Tara asked Eric, as a way of announcing that she was now open for business.

"Something to help me pass this next math test," Eric said with a grimace.

"You know the math," Tara told him. "You just have to stay calm."

"I know," Eric said, sighing. "It's just so hard with all those questions staring at me."

"All right," Tara said, thinking. "Payment is going to be five minutes of meditation every night this week. Just before you go to bed."

"I can't," Eric said, starting to sound panicked. "I can't—"

"Yes, you can," Tara said firmly. She caught the boy's hand and made him look at her. "You can learn how to breathe deeply at your father's house."

Eric wrinkled his nose.

Tara knew Eric's fear was irrational, that he'd take in too much of the air in his father's house and would somehow become more like him, an alcoholic who was at least functioning, unlike Eric's mom who was in prison.

"Remember, meditation isn't just about taking in the air, but also about releasing it. You can let go of everything you take in, every molecule of air," Tara said. "Maybe you should focus on that."

"Huh. I hadn't thought of that," Eric said. He considered the payment she was asking while Tara went ahead and put together the most calming elements she knew and started her tea.

"Fine," Eric said after a few more moments. "I'll meditate for five minutes every night before going to sleep, concentrating on releasing the air, not just bringing it in."

"Good," Tara said. The water had just started to boil. "Let this steep for five minutes," she said handing the cup to him. "And bring it back when you've finished. I've given you enough for two cups."

"Thanks," Eric said with a grateful smile. He took a deep sniff of herbs. "Chamomile, mint, and lavender?"

"Close," Tara said, impressed that he'd gotten all that just from the smell before tasting it. "Gingko, too," she said.

"Ah," Eric said, nodding. "I'll have to remember that."

He turned and went back to where he'd been studying, and the next customer came up, a pre-teen girl with beautiful black skin and her hair braided tightly in rows across her head. Tara gave her a tea with borage and other herbs to boost her self-confidence. For "payment," she wanted the girl to remember to use her twenty seconds of courage and do something she wouldn't normally do the next day.

All through the afternoon, the people in the community center would come up and ask Tara for different teas. Teruko stretched out in front of the containers of herbs, purring loudly sometimes to catch someone's attention, getting scritches as the person talked with Tara of their need.

Many of the teas Tara made were just tasty ingredients mixed together with a deft hand. While the ingredients did have medicinal properties, Tara was aware that for them to work the person would have to make tea from them on a regular basis, not just a couple times a week when she came to the shelter. That was the way of herbs—they didn't work immediately, and generally weren't as potent as modern medicine.

Sometimes, though, as she picked out the herbs she felt a spark pass through her, flowing out of her fingers and into the tea. She knew that her hedgewitch magic had just engaged and the tea would be extra effective.

By the time the community shelter closed up for the night, around eight PM, Tara felt exhausted, as she knew she would. But she didn't feel drained. It was always a weird energy, and she felt both wired and tired, as if she'd consumed too much caffeine after staying up all night.

Fortunately, she had both a long ride on the MAX, along with a long walk, before she'd arrive at the house she shared. That would help her relax before she tried sleeping. Plus, once she got home she'd make herself a nice tea.

The empty streets held an orange glow from the streetlights. It was misting out, not raining, the air full of moisture. Flowers had been in bloom for a while. Tara was looking forward to the lilacs that would start blooming soon, followed by the roses. Cars raced past her, hurrying to their important destinations.

Every once in a while, Tara thought about getting a car. But it would be such a huge expense. She'd arranged her life so that it was easy for her to get everywhere via public transportation. One big triangle, with Hallowed Ground to the north, the Y to the south and east, and her home to the south and west.

Soot suddenly appeared beside her. Tara didn't hear footsteps behind her, but normally, the tamed wind wouldn't walk her home unless there was some danger.

Tara stopped and looked back. It took her a moment to recognize the figure walking toward her. The cane gave him away, however. Lucius was following her.

On the one hand, Lucius was currently part of her coven and regularly performed magic with Tara and the others. On the other hand, Lucius wasn't human, but a being of power.

Tara still didn't know exactly what Lucius was. She knew that many of the myths of the elves were based off of encounters with his kind. He was completely alien. Fortunately, he wore a "mask" of humanity, so that unsettling difference was hidden most of the time.

"Hi, Lucius," Tara said as he stepped closer. He was about six feet tall, with thick silver hair that hung down past his shoulders. His face looked pale, long, and angular in the streetlights, giving him a more otherworldly appearance. The light was too dim for her to see his brilliant blue eyes, and tonight they seemed much darker and brooding. He wore an elegant double-breasted black coat that hung down past his knees. Water had beaded up across the shoulders, giving Lucius his own glow.

Lucius didn't address her, but looked down at Soot. "Why did you have to warn her?" he asked. He had a slight British accent and was unbelievably old. He'd come to the New World "as a lark" centuries before.

Soot gave the equivalent of a doggie laugh, sitting

his butt down on the ground beside Tara and leaning against her leg.

Tara read the dog's response to be something along the lines of, "She's my mistress. What's it to you?"

"Never mind," Lucius told the dog before looking back up at Tara. "You received one of those nastygrams again this morning, right? Boating accident?"

Tara nodded. Again, she didn't see what the Riprap man's point was. She was not responsible.

"Have any of the missives you've received been about the harbor wall?"

"No," Tara said. "Just the deaths on the river."

Lucius heaved a great sigh. "Believe it or not, I'm starting to wonder if those notes from your nightmare man are just a decoy."

"What do you mean?" Tara asked, surprised.

"The Riprap man wants you focused on the deaths in the river, and feeling guilty, rather than paying attention to the rest of the river system and what's happening in the big picture."

"Okay," Tara said slowly. That seemed like a lot of work on the part of the Riprap man. Yet again, it had been effective. She hadn't been paying any attention to anything else regarding the river. "So…what are you saying? That there's a problem with the seawall?"

"There was a tremendous amount of snow this winter, up in the mountains," Lucius said. "Plus, that long freeze at the end of February."

Tara nodded. It had been colder and snowier all winter long, even in the city.

"We're possibly facing massive flooding as the snow melts," Lucius warned. "If we get another of those so quaintly called 'pineapple express' storms. We could see another flood, similar to what happened in 1996."

Tara couldn't contain her gasp. "But I thought the Riprap man wanted to protect Portland!"

"I think he did, before you broke his connection to the river," Lucius said.

Tara didn't bother pointing out that it wasn't necessarily her who'd broken the connection between the Riprap man and the river spirit Mulinohana. She'd been the decoy while the coven itself destroyed their bond.

"Now, who knows what he wants?" Lucius said. "He may have decided that the best way to get back at you is to destroy Portland, then blame you for it."

Tara gave an exasperated sigh. That sounded like so many of the spiteful men she'd run across over the years. "Swell," she finally said. She shivered. The night had grown colder while they'd talked, the mist heavier. It would soon ease over into rain. "So…what now? Should I have Richard look up problems with the seawall?"

"Yes, exactly," Lucius said. He sounded relieved. "And flood predictions for this spring."

Tara couldn't help but tease Lucius a little. "You know, you could ask him to do it yourself."

The look of horror mixed with disgust that crossed Lucius's face was priceless. While on the one hand, Lucius respected the results Richard brought the group, he also distanced himself from the research librarian as much as possible, so that Richard wouldn't be tempted to start researching *him*. Though Tara knew that Richard had already looked into Lucius as much as he possibly could without the other being knowing about it.

After a moment, Lucius composed himself again. "Oh, and one other thing."

He paused, seemingly lost in thought, until Tara prompted him. "And that is?"

"Like the bridges, I suspect that your friend the Riprap man did something to help protect the harbor wall," Lucius said slowly. "However, I doubt he used a witch's heart."

"Then what did he use?" Tara asked, puzzled.

Lucius hesitated. "I doubt that he was able to use one of my kind. But it wasn't a normal sacrifice."

"How do you know that?" Tara said, surprised.

Lucius merely shrugged.

She couldn't help but roll her eyes at his non-helpfulness. "How is Richard supposed to find out about something like that? Human deaths might at least be reported."

"I know," Lucius said. He shook his head. "We might need to go visit the spirit buried at the base of the seawall, however."

Tara felt all the blood leave her face. "Miss Lucy gave me a potion to go visit one of the witches at the base of the Morrison bridge," she said. The potion had been awful to take. Sludge mixed with rotten seaweed, and that was after oregano had been added to sweeten the taste. Her chest grew tight and she pushed down on the feeling of bile rising up.

"We'd do it differently, this time," Lucius assured her. "We might want to consider doing it on the coming equinox."

"Why?" Tara asked. "What could that spirit tell us? It isn't as if the Riprap man will make another sacrifice. He's no longer connected to the river."

"He may not be able to help himself," Lucius said. "Once a man gets a taste for the hunt, a taste for blood, it's difficult for him to let go. And the Riprap man has been killing for a long, long time."

"I didn't think of that," Tara said slowly. She was going to have to make sure that Richard expanded his search, to see if a woman had committed suicide on the winter solstice the year before. While the Riprap man hadn't been bothering her, that didn't mean he hadn't gone after someone else.

Was the Riprap man part of the reason why so many people jumped off the bridges in Portland? Was he blaming her for all the bodies pulled from the river, even though he'd been causing the deaths himself?

"Oh, I so didn't need to start worrying about this tonight," Tara said after a bit.

"I could make sure you had sweet dreams," Lucius said, his voice growing deeper, into that late-night-jazz announcer territory, sounding like smooth sex.

Tara held herself stiffly. This wasn't the first time that Lucius had propositioned her. She knew that he had, in the past, been intimate with Kyle, her best friend. They weren't exclusive, however, and Kyle had spent one awkward evening trying to explain to Tara that she was free to take Lucius up on his suggestions.

But that felt wrong to Tara. Particularly as she was the head of their coven. Being physically intimate with any of them would throw off their balance of power.

As Lucius appeared to still be waiting for an answer, Tara finally told him, "No, thank you. I will get myself home and make myself some tea."

"Your loss," Lucius said with a negligent wave of

his hand. "I will see you on Monday," he said, turning and walking away, quickly disappearing in the mist.

Soot nudged Tara's leg, getting her to look down at him. He gave her a doggie eye roll, then got up and turned around, walking again toward the MAX stop.

Tara followed the tamed wind after a moment. She was never sure what Soot's relationship with Lucius was. The wind always seemed more *aware* around the other being.

At least Teruko hadn't suddenly appeared, draped across Tara's shoulders like a living stole, expecting to be carried home. Then again, the mist was getting a lot heavier. Probably the only reason the cat hadn't shown up was because she didn't want to get her fur wet.

Tara felt more tired now as she walked toward the train stop. She didn't know if she was in danger or not. Or if the danger was now to the entire city of Portland. She was going to have to get Richard to do some serious research.

In the meanwhile, time for home, tea, and bed.

CHAPTER 2

I continue to meditate and consider my options for marking the seawall as sacred to the river god. While it would be possible to find a hedgewitch with a menagerie of familiars, it would be difficult to sacrifice all of them, as they're merely elements and don't have a "life" of their own. Possibly I could acquire an entire coven of witches, bind their hearts up and down the length of the wall, but that solution strikes me as too messy. I need a more elegant solution. I've asked the river god what He would prefer, but his answer wasn't satisfying, and presents me with another puzzle. "Find another Being."

Wilson Evermore, Civil Magician and Protector of Portland, 1925

"THE HARBOR WALL IS COLLAPSING," RICHARD announced when Tara called him the next day on her lunch break. She'd sent Richard an email the night before, telling him about Lucius's warnings.

"And good afternoon to you too," Tara said. She sighed. She'd been teaching at the Y all morning, filling in for one of the yoga instructors who'd called in sick. Tara would spend the afternoon teaching her swimming classes.

Currently, Tara sat alone in the staff breakroom. The smell of the tangerines from her lunch conflicted with the artificial scent of the lemon wax used on the gym floor next door. The room itself was maybe nine feet by six, with a round table in the center that had seen better days, the wooden top all scratched and scuffed. The countertops hadn't fared any better, and the gray material was stained in many places, including large yellow stains from what had probably been turmeric-loaded lunches. A silent TV hanging from the far corner showed the news, the rolling marquee at the bottom of the screen a constant commentary on what was happening in the world, most of it depressing and bad.

"The problems with the harbor wall aren't necessarily public knowledge," Richard said, sounding angry. "The city has commissioned some studies, then tried to hide the results. They're hoping that they can get by a few more years before they have to do any actual work on it."

"Okay," Tara said. "What does that mean, though? Is it going to collapse tomorrow? Later this spring if we get a heavy rain? Or in a couple years?"

"The wall wasn't supposed to last a hundred years," Richard said. "It's been eroding for a while. However, the city voted to put more tax dollars toward fixing the roads."

"Yeah, that makes sense," Tara said, nodding. That would actually be popular with more voters. Plus, if the harbor wall has been holding for a long while, why bother fixing it now?

"However, the confluence of events that caused the 1996 flood aren't unique to that year," Richard said. "All the events that happened that year, like the heavy snows up river and the surprising freeze that occurred at the end of February have both happened this year, in record amounts. All we'd need is a really warm, heavy rain for a flood to occur."

"Would the wall hold up if it got hit by a flood?" Tara asked, trying to follow along.

Richard sighed. "Possibly? No one knows." He paused, then added, "Unless there's something to Lucius's claim that someone, or something, other than a witch was used to bind the wall."

"Not sure I'm following you," Tara said.

"If the wall got hit with a wall of water, it would start to gradually give way. It wouldn't just explode. That only happens in Hollywood with good CGI," Richard explained. "You know that the seawall is haunted, right?"

"I didn't, actually, Tara said. "Truly haunted? Or just tourist trap haunted?" There were such things as ghosts and spirits, but they didn't normally interact with the living. They could be called by a strong witch or her coven.

"You're going to have to tell me that, actually," Richard said. "However, there have been legends of ghosts up and down that wall since it was first constructed. Or rather, a ghost. Tall and thin, willowy, with long silver hair."

"Lucius said it wasn't one of his kind who got taken," Tara said. "But I wonder if it's a relative of a sort."

"According to the legends, she's a siren, and has called men to their death. I haven't actually been able to find any deaths related to her, at least not in the neighborhoods that she supposedly haunts."

"She might just be placing the suggestion, so that the person goes to the nearest bridge and jumps off," Tara speculated.

"Great. Supernatural serial killers. Just what we need," Richard groused. "As if the Pacific Northwest doesn't already have enough."

That made Tara smile, at least. While Seattle seemed to be the home for more serial killers per capita than any other city, Portland still had its share.

"I also thought of something else." He cleared his throat. "What if the flood waters start rising and she finally has a chance to destroy the harbor wall? Instead of luring just a few to their deaths, she can kill thousands?"

Tara took a deep breath. "I don't know if that's possible. But Lucius said that we're going to have to visit the spirit who lives at the base of the harbor wall. Possibly on the equinox."

"Oh," Richard said. "Can you at least promise to tell me all the details? Afterward?"

"Of course," Tara said. As Richard was fully mundane, he had no idea of what happened when the coven performed magic together.

"One more thing. A woman did jump to her death on

the winter solstice last year. People thought she on something because she'd seemed so out of it. The police have closed the case, ruling it a suicide. They claim that she was depressed, not that she was drunk, so her tox screen had probably come back negative."

"That implies that the Riprap man might still be killing," Tara said. How was she going to stop him, if it was indeed him?

"Possibly," Richard said. "I've been trying to link the bodies in the river to possible suicides that he might have caused, but I haven't had any luck. He did *not* send you a newspaper clipping about Margo, the woman who committed suicide on the solstice last year."

"Huh," Tara said. Maybe he was taking responsibility for some of the people who'd died.

"But the number of deaths from suicide is disturbing," Richard said. "We're much higher than we should be for this time of the year."

"Could that be the river spirit?" Tara said.

"Hell if I know," Richard said. "The economy kind of sucks and the political climate isn't giving people hope. It could just be circumstantial."

"Right," Tara said, knowing that Richard was trying to make her feel better. However, she still had a niggling doubt that somehow, Mulinohana, the spirit of the river, was causing these deaths.

"I'll send you what I've found so far," Richard said. "You still coming over for dinner Saturday night?"

"That's tomorrow night, right?" Tara asked. She had a retail-like schedule, and Sundays were her actual Friday, with Mondays and Tuesdays off.

"Yup," Richard said. "Jeannie is looking forward to hanging out."

"Cool," Tara said. Though Richard and Jeannie were now living together, they'd made an effort to invite people over for dinner on a regular basis. "No surprises, though, right?"

"None," Richard said. "Wouldn't make that mistake again."

People who were couples tended to look at single people like Tara as a problem to fix. She'd endured their "surprise" guest who'd showed up for dinner once.

"What should I bring?"

"Just yourself," Richard insisted.

Tara smiled. He and Jeannie wouldn't ever allow her to bring anything for dinner, but they would gladly accept any tea that she made for them. She'd be sure to bring a few ounces of something for them to enjoy.

"So…are we going to tell her?" Richard asked after a few moments of awkward silence.

"Is it time?" Tara asked. Richard had been formally invited to be part of the coven, and knew about witches and magic, even though he was completely mundane. He kept the information to himself, even after he and Jeannie had moved in together.

"I don't know," Richard said after a few moments. "But…but it might be."

"I leave that decision up to you," Tara said. Both Tara and the rest of the coven had already approved of him telling Jeannie when the time came.

"I don't know," Richard said, whining.

Tara couldn't help but roll her eyes. Richard had always struck her as commitment-phobic. It had surprised her when he'd moved in with Jeannie after knowing her for such a short period of time.

"Do you want to marry her?" Tara asked quietly. "Spend the rest of your life with her?"

"Maybe?" Richard said. "I can't imagine living without her."

"You've said that before," Tara reminded him. "Are those just words? Just your comfort speaking? Or do you truly feel it?"

Richard gave a heavy sigh.

"I'm going back to work," Tara announced. "Give you more time to stew on things."

"Thanks. I think," Richard said.

"Talk to you later, see you on Friday," Tara said, swiping the phone off.

There really wasn't anything she could do for Richard. He'd have to make his own decision, sooner or later. She understood his hesitation though. What if he told Jeannie about the witches and the coven and she decided to leave? It was pretty weird.

But Jeannie was also a Portland native. Tara had faith that she'd take any additional weirdness in stride.

TARA DREAMED OF FLOODS THAT NIGHT. A WALL OF water was traveling down river, heading toward Portland. It towered above her, at least thirty feet tall. The water roared as it gained speed. Storm winds blew from the river, carrying icy sleet that stung her bare arms. The air smelled of the iron cold of winter storms. Dark clouds loomed ominously above her.

Tara raced to get in front of the wall. In the perfect logic of dreams, she believed that if she could get in front of the water, she could stop it.

She was somewhere north of the city. She could just see the city in the distance, the taller buildings and bridges shimmering and looking frail through the spray of water the wall generated.

Tara ran along a rutted dirt road on the river bank, with tufted green grass growing down the center of it. She managed to avoid the rocks and puddles that could have tripped her. However, people kept getting in her way. Slow walking couples who held hands and blocked the entire way. A giggling group of teenage girls who yelled insults at Tara when she pushed by them. Even a young man walking a group of a dozen dogs.

At the edge of a park, Tara grabbed a bicycle (a mode of transport that she never enjoyed). She finally was almost caught up with the edge of the water when a warning bleet caused her to pause.

Really? A herd of sheep?

Tara abandoned the river path and ran to the nearest street. Though she didn't know how to drive, she still stole an old truck. The streets were too far away from the river, though, so she cut across a wild variety of yards and meadows, finally able to roar down the dirt path.

Finally, Tara got in front of the water. She leaped out of the car and sprinted across the water, standing firmly in front of the wave.

"STOP!" Tara yelled, her hands out in front of her, all her magic focused forward. She built a large magical forcefield all around her, a bubble of safety.

The water didn't bother to even pause. It flowed around her safety bubble, parting like a curtain, leaving her standing behind it as it destroyed the city.

Tara woke up stiff and sore. Every muscle was tired

as if she'd actually been running that much. Her jaw ached from how hard she'd clenched her teeth all night.

It was just a nightmare. There was no wall of water heading for Portland.

After a long hot shower, Tara finally read her email from Richard.

Which was all about the 1996 flood, how the weather had been similar that year, and how record rainfall was predicted for the following week.

TARA DRAGGED THROUGH HER MORNING, TEACHING AT the Y. On the weekend, Hallowed Ground would get a lot more volunteers, people who worked regular hours during the week, so they didn't really need her. The Y, though, had classes all day.

She still managed to find all the energy the young ones needed, her first class. It was the most difficult class for Tara to teach sometimes, not because the kids were bad, but because it was so early.

Between classes, Tara made herself an extra strong cup of tea from an already prepared bag. She'd started with a base of a lovely Assam black tea, then she'd added Ginkgo Biloba, apple mint, hibiscus, and dried lemon peel. It was a really bright tasting tea, guaranteed to wake her up. Though she'd already had her caffeine before her first class, she knew that a second dose wouldn't hurt.

The rest of the day went by swimmingly, as it were. Despite her nightmare of chasing after a wall of water, Tara still loved the water. This was her home. This was where she felt most comfortable.

However, teaching all day left her tired, particularly after her poor sleep the night before. She decided to call it an early evening with Richard and Jeannie. They'd understand if she just ate and headed out soon afterward.

Though Richard had offered to come and pick Tara up at the Y, she didn't take him up on his offer. Instead, she took the MAX, then a bus up Foster. The traffic moved slowly, impeded by the construction.

It didn't make any sense to her why the city had decided to narrow the busy artery down to a single lane in each direction. Yes, it would be prettier. But the traffic was already atrocious. Making the streets harder to navigate wasn't about to cut down on the number of cars.

But she wasn't in charge. All she could do was sit and fume as the bus lumbered along from one stop to the next.

A change in the air of the bus made her look away from the construction outside.

Crap.

The Riprap man stood in the aisle of the bus, close to the rear exit. He looked far worse than the last time she'd seen him. He still wore his old bowler hat and trousers, but no jacket, and his shirt hung in tatters. His exposed torso appeared to be listing to one side, the rocks that made up his body bulging in first one direction, then the other.

What was he doing here? Why was he here? Was he coming for her again next week, during the spring equinox?

He glared at her from where he stood. His face was clear, and it no longer seemed as though he peered at her from under the water. His eyes appeared to be black holes, sunk deep above gaunt cheeks. He still had what she would call a weak chin, soft and undefined. She couldn't see his teeth, but the way his cheeks had sunk reminded her of the older homeless people who didn't have dentures.

She heard the words echo through the air, though she knew he hadn't spoken them out loud. "Your fault. You're to blame." He pointed an accusatory finger in her direction.

Tara felt the terror of the wall of water crashing toward the city from her nightmare the night before. The smell of the river and its marshes washed over her. Chills cascaded down her arms and her spine. She heard a dull boom as the harbor wall exploded, the waters cackling madly as they raced beyond their hated man-made borders.

"Your fault."

The bus drew to a stop and the Riprap man got off, disappearing as soon as he touched the sidewalk.

Tara shivered again, swallowing down the bile that had suddenly risen in her throat.

Richard thought there might be a flood soon.

The Riprap man was going to guarantee it.

Tara pushed back from the table with a replete sigh. "That was wonderful," she said yet again. Jeannie had gone all out that night, making a rolled pork roast that had blueberries, thyme, sage, and rosemary in the center of it, the perfect combination of sweet and savory. She'd served roasted root vegetables on the side

—turnips, radishes, and rutabagas—cooked with pecans and hazelnuts to sweeten them. Desert would be a lemon tart that barely had any sugar in it, in an almond-meal crust.

Tara knew better than to believe it was all for her. Jeannie loved to cook. She'd actually considered going into culinary school when she'd graduated college ten years before. However, she'd quickly discovered that she didn't want to turn her hobby into a profession. Instead, she happily invited friends over as it gave her an excuse to try new recipes and show off.

"I'm glad you liked it," Jeannie said with a happy smile. She was a petite woman, barely five foot two, with sandy-brown hair that she wore just past her shoulders. Despite her love of eating, Jeannie was very slim. She regularly fasted, eating only one meal per day, making that meal a feast. Like Tara, Jeannie didn't eat a lot of grains, but focused instead on healthy proteins with lots of veggies.

One of the agreements that Jeannie and Richard had quickly reached was that while Jeannie did the cooking, Richard did the cleaning. He was actually proud of the fact that Jeannie had never cleaned a single pot or plate. Period. No matter if she did the cooking or not.

Tara smiled as Richard grabbed Jeannie's hand and kissed the back of it. "Thank you," he said sincerely. She'd seen him do this before, to always express gratitude and mean it. He didn't toss the words off casually.

He really was in love with Jeannie. Tara could see it in his eyes, the way he looked at her. It made her feel warm inside, to be around such love.

Maybe someday she'd find that as well...but she

honestly wasn't looking for it at this point. She had too good of a life, too much to do, to want to be weighed down by a relationship.

And that attitude was exactly why she shouldn't get involved with anyone in the first place. Not until she stopped seeing it as a burden and more as part of her support network.

Tara rose from her seat and started carrying dishes away from the table. Richard seemed to come back to himself, tearing his eyes away from Jeannie and standing himself.

"Sit," Tara said firmly. "Entertain your girlfriend. I'll carry the dishes away and make tea."

Richard sat with a loud oouuufff. "If you insist," he said with a lazy smile.

Tara was glad that they'd been able to remain friends after they'd dated. She was also glad that he'd found Jeannie, who was obviously perfect for him. He had a few more silver hairs running through his black hair and he actually looked older now than when she'd first met him, more mature than he used to be. That didn't mean he still didn't have an extremely goofy side. That night he wore a T-shirt with the slogan, "Because...SCIENCE!"

They'd been sitting around a small card table that had been set up in the middle of the living room, with the TV on one side and the couch of doom on the other (once you slid into the soft cushions, it was deceptively difficult to get back out). A sliding glass door opening up onto a patio was at the far end of the room. On the other side, a tall island separated the huge kitchen from the rest of the space, an open floor plan that Tara actually approved of.

She carried their plates and the leftovers from the table, taking her time as they chatted about Jeannie's next planned meal—a feast for their board game night the following week. She took it as a challenge to make gourmet finger food, as they wouldn't be sitting down for a complete meal.

Tara let their words fade into the background as she started preparing their tea for the night. Both Richard and Jeannie drank coffee, so Tara had made up a few ounces of a heavier tea for them. It started with a rooibos base (as it was late at night and they all needed decaf), then added chicory root, dandelion roots, barley, cacao nibs, as well as some dried vanilla. To the cups she added a touch of powdered dark chocolate.

When she walked back into the living room, cups in hand, she realized that she should have paid a bit more attention while she'd been making the tea.

The conversation had obviously turned serious in her absence. It felt like walking into the middle of a sermon.

Tara silently served each of them a mug of tea, then went back and fetched the cream and sugar.

The air felt sticky with anticipation. Tara felt like taking off the sweater she was wearing, as she suddenly felt overly warm.

"What's up?" Tara asked after she sat down.

Jeannie stared at Richard while Richard focused on his cup of tea for a few moments. He cleared his throat. "I have something to tell Jeannie," he said slowly.

"Okay," Tara said, nodding. "You can do this."

Richard sighed, taking a quick sip of his tea before turning back to Jeannie. "You know I love you, right?" he said, reaching out for her hand.

"Yes, but you're scaring me. Those words are usually followed by some sort of 'but,'" she said sharply.

At least she did take Richard's hand. Tara took that as a good sign. Richard clung to it like a lifeline.

"I have something to tell you. Something for Tara to show you. I need you to know this, about this part of my life," Richard said. "It is private, though. You can't ever, ever, tell anyone about this."

Jeannie looked from Richard to Tara, who nodded. "He's right. It isn't your secret to tell or to share."

Surprise crossed Jeannie's face. "Okay," she said slowly. "Now you're both scaring me."

"It isn't scary. Or rather, not that scary," Richard said, trying to reassure her. He cleared his throat. "You know that I get together with Tara and the gang on Monday nights, right?"

"Right," Jeannie said, nodding. "It's an eclectic group. You meet at Hallowed Ground, that homeless shelter. Do your volunteer work."

"It's more than that," Richard admitted.

"So you're having orgies," Jeannie said.

"No," Richard said firmly.

Tara couldn't help grin. He'd done the same thing to her when she'd tried to tell him about being a witch.

"Really? That's too bad. Lucius is quite a looker. I'd imagine he'd be rather...intense in bed," Jeannie said with a teasing grin.

Tara snorted. It wouldn't have surprised her in the least if Lucius had propositioned not only Richard but Jeannie the few times he'd met her. That was exactly his speed.

"We're not having sex," Richard said. "We're doing magic."

Jeannie peered at him, puzzled. "Like…how?"

"We're a coven of witches," Richard said. "I don't have any magic," he quickly assured Jeannie. "I've just been invited to participate."

"A coven?" Jeannie asked. She turned to look at Tara. "I suppose you're part of this."

"It's my coven," Tara said firmly. "I put it together."

"And you believe that you do magic," Jeannie said, glancing from Tara to Richard and back again.

"Yes," Tara said.

"Show me," Jeannie said. She sat back in her chair and crossed her arms over her chest.

Tara tilted her head to one side, studying Jeannie. She seemed angry. Tara wasn't sure why.

"All right," Tara said. She pushed her chair back from the table and stood. "Just remember, you can't ever tell anyone about this."

Jeannie snorted. "No one would believe me."

Tara shook her head. This was not going to end well. She could tell.

Still, she'd promised Richard that she'd show Jeannie her magic if they ever got around to telling her.

"Do you remember my dog Soot?" Tara said.

Jeannie nodded. She didn't care much for dogs.

Hopefully, that wouldn't stop Soot from showing up.

Tara gave a long whistle, her usual call for the tamed wind to show up.

Jeannie gasped as Soot materialized out of thin air, sitting at Tara's feet, looking up.

"Fetch," Tara said. She held in her mind the clear image of a daffodil, one of the ones that grew in the gardens at the base of the condo. She hated having to pick one of the flowers there; however, she needed to be able to show Jeannie exactly where the flower had come from if she should ask.

Soot nodded and flowed out the closed glass door of the balcony.

Jeannie sat stiffly in her chair, her arms tighter across her chest, hugging herself in fear.

After a few moments, Soot flowed back through the glass, placing a long daffodil at Tara's feet. "Good boy," Tara said, praising the wind and patting his smooth head. She picked up the flower and put it on the table in front of Jeannie.

"Home," Tara told Soot.

He whined at her. He was bored. He wanted something more to do.

Tara had seen a homeless encampment set up along a street near here. She held the place firmly in her mind. "Comfort those you can," she said softly.

Soot nodded and vanished.

Tara turned to Jeannie who still stared at the daffodil on the table as if it were a poisonous snake about to bite her. "Do you want to see more?" she asked quietly.

"No," Jeannie said firmly. She finally looked up, fixing her glare on Tara. "I believe you."

"But?" Richard asked.

"If you can do this magic, why haven't you healed the world?" Jeannie asked. "There's so much that's wrong. So many places broken down. So much hurt and evil. Magic should be able to stop all of that. Why haven't you?"

Tara sighed and sat down at the table. "There's only so much we can do," she said softly. "We do try to heal the world. To bring peace to troubled souls. To clean up the messes others leave behind. There aren't enough of us, though. And I don't have endless energy."

"I see," Jeannie said, still angry.

"Plus, not all witches seek the betterment of others," Tara felt she had to add. "Some seek their own selfish goals."

Jeannie gave an expressive sigh at that. "Of course," she said. "Human nature, right?"

"Exactly," Tara said.

"What magic can you do?" Jeannie said, turning her burning gaze on Richard.

"I can't do magic," Richard assured her. "Nothing beyond my mad researching skills."

"You can't? Or you can't show me?" Jeannie asked. She still sounded hostile.

"I don't have magic," Richard said.

"He's completely mundane," Tara added. "Doesn't have any magic at all." She'd been hoping that possibly, after being involved in a few circles of power, that he might start to show a spark. He still had no magic at all, though Lucius claimed that Richard did have a primitive power that he was able to add to the circle, though it was completely undisciplined.

"I don't believe you," Jeannie said. "Why, if you're so powerful, do you need him? Why not invite other people instead?"

"He does have mad researching skills," Tara said. "And I need those. We're kind of a renegade coven. I don't have access to the books of lore that the other covens have."

Jeannie just shook her head. "You could use those skills without making him part of all…this."

Tara wasn't exactly sure what she meant by "all this." "True," Tara said. "And I gave him that option. I wanted him to be a part of the circles, though."

"I need to think about this," Jeannie said, pushing herself up to standing. "You get the couch tonight," she told Richard firmly as she marched off toward their shared bedroom, closing the door behind her firmly.

Richard looked as though he'd been kicked in the gut. "Sorry about that," he said after a few moments.

"Don't be," Tara said. She sighed. "Hopefully you'll be able to bring her around."

Somehow, she doubted it. Jeannie appeared to have some real prejudices against witches, or those with power. Richard associating with such people, despite having no power himself, seemed to just add insult to injury.

Richard gave Tara a watery smile. "Give you a ride home?"

Tara accepted gratefully. They didn't talk much on the ride home, and as expected, Tara had further nightmares that evening, only this time, after the flood waters took out most of the city, the ghosts of the dead came after her.

CHAPTER 3

I have finally discovered what could be a solution to my dilemma about the wall. The witches, while powerful, are sedentary. They don't travel far, except to consort with each other. For the wall I need a creature who will roam up and down the entire entity. Though I did not originally believe it, there appear to be beings who are not human, beings of great power, who walk among the humans in disguise. I have been learning how to recognize such creatures. There is one race known to the others as the Travelers. They are rare, extremely solitary, and do not stay in a single location for very long. I will have to find one of those, trap its soul and bind it to the sea wall. And I must hurry. The start of construction draws near.

Wilson Evermore, Hunter and Protector, 1927.

THE HAPPY SHOUTS OF CHILDREN PLAYING IN THE WATER echoed off the tall ceiling of the pool. Tara stood at the shallow end of the warm water, holding up one of the younger ones while he kicked hard, learning how to better propel himself. He almost had the hang of it—it was more a matter of coordination than anything else.

Finally, a loud buzzer sounded, announcing the end of the hour. Tara blew on the whistle she wore clipped to the shoulder of her red bathing suit. "Time!" she shouted.

Though she didn't consciously add magic to make herself sound louder, her wild magic caused it to happen anyway, her voice booming across the room. Tara knew if she really tried, she could shout loud enough to cause the water to ripple.

As it was, all the kids stopped playing abruptly, the silence itself shocking.

"Time," Tara called again, this time in a normal voice.

The kids started making regular kid-like noises again as they splashed their way to the side of the pool, hauling themselves out and heading toward either their parents who sat around the edges of the pool, or the locker rooms.

"Thank you, Ms. Tara!" several of them called, waving after they'd gotten out of the pool.

"See you next week!" she said in return.

Gradually, the pool room emptied. Tara checked the clock. Did she have time to do a few laps on her own before she hit the locker room herself? Probably.

She grinned and dove into the water, pulling herself forward with hard strokes, aiming for the far end of the pool.

Though she always expected the Riprap man to bother her here, when she was in the water, he never showed up. It finally occurred to her that while the Riprap man had been bound to a water spirit, he himself was an earth spirit. It made much more sense for him to bother her on solid ground than in the water. Or on trains, that were like bridges, not set in a single location but spanning more than one.

Still, Tara felt as though the water started pushing against her as she began her second lap. She stubbornly swam on as the water grew heavier, denser. Finally, panting, Tara reached the end of the lane and popped up above the water.

The lights flickered. The comforting smell of chlorine that always said *home* to Tara was replaced with the smell of the river, damp and fecund. Tara shivered as the water around her grew cold.

High up, near the ceiling, storm clouds gathered. What fresh hell was this? This wasn't the Riprap man, that much Tara knew. Lightning raced across the darkness in streaks. Winds howled furiously, itching to take apart anything that stood in their path. Tara shivered as the temperature dropped.

The air changed abruptly. A strange, warm wind blew around her, then raced up, challenging the colder winds above. Tara smelled rain. If the storm continued, Tara knew that it wouldn't be drops of rain falling. No, it would land in sheets of water, as if buckets were being dumped.

Just as quickly as it had come, the storm vanished, leaving Tara breathless.

She couldn't shake the feeling that she'd just had a

vision of what was coming: a massive storm guaranteed to flood all of Portland.

Trembling, Tara pulled herself from the pool. Her muscles ached as if she'd done an hour's worth of laps. She quickly toweled off and headed toward the locker rooms.

How long had she been in the pool? Most of the kids and their parents were long gone. Just a couple of teenagers remained, blow drying their hair and gossiping. She snuck a quick peek at the clock.

Holy cow. Forty-five minutes had passed without her realizing it. Had she been actually at the edge of the pool that entire time? Or had she been swimming?

Tara headed for the showers. It took a long while for the hot water to soak through her chilled skin and into her bones.

A storm was brewing, heading for the city. She'd check the weather reports, but it honestly wouldn't matter what they said.

Richard had said that all the other pieces were already in place, replicating what had happened in 1996. All they needed was a really heavy, warm rain.

She was going to have to find a way to control the river, stop it from smashing against the harbor wall and probably destroying it, flooding the city.

But how?

~

"WHAT ABOUT MARIGOLD PETALS?" TARA ASKED AS Ginny perused Tara's shelves, looking for the perfect element to balance out her Irish morning breakfast tea. They stood in the kitchen that Tara shared with the rest of her flatmates. It was late Sunday evening, and though Tara felt especially tired, she hadn't cancelled her meeting with the other hedgewitch. She had too many questions. Besides, Monday was actually the start of her weekend, and she'd be able to sleep in.

"Aye, that might do," Ginny said, reaching unerringly for the glass jelly jar.

It gave Tara an insight into how she must appear to others as she made up her own teas, never hesitating, the jars occasionally leaping into her hand when she raised it.

It was a good reminder to her that she had to be extra careful when her flatmates were around, so they wouldn't start questioning her like Richard had.

Ginny felt as though she belonged here. Then again, that seemed to be one of her knacks, to always fit in everywhere she went. She'd let her bright red curls grow out some, to keep her head warmer during the cold months, but she still shaved the edges of her head, giving herself a floppy mohawk. She'd recently gotten her left eyebrow pierced with a gold ring to match the one she wore in her right nostril, making her look more balanced, though her green eyes and wide smile still promised all kinds of mischief. She wore a comfortable bulky sweater in a color that Tara would call oatmeal, as well as black leggings that had geometric patterns in white. They matched the tattoos that Ginny had running from behind her ears and down her neck, connected triangles and octagons.

Tara sometimes felt like the uncoolest witch in Portland, especially compared to Ginny and the others. She wore her straight brown hair pulled back in a ponytail, and tonight wore a comfortable dark gray sweatshirt over light gray sweatpants. The only color she had were tall slipper socks in red, gold, black, and blue.

She leaned against a counter as she watched Ginny work her own magic putting together her own concoction. The kitchen was warm and empty, just the two of them. In the living room, the TV blared a soccer match that Erin had recorded earlier.

Ginny gave Tara a grin over her shoulder when Erin exploded in loud cheers. "'Tis a good house, here," she said, nodding.

Tara agreed. "Good mix of people, too." A musician, a writer with a day job, and two travelers who needed someplace cheap to live so they could save money and go on their next great adventure. They all took care of the house, the chores divided between them. They had monthly dinners, followed by their house meeting and airing of grievances.

As a result, the kitchen was generally clean, everyone taking care of their own dishes and cleanup, the floors washed once a week. The space was large and inviting, with a gourmet stove with six burners, a huge farm sink, and plenty of counterspace. There wasn't enough refrigerator space, so Tara had invested in a small fridge that she kept in her room.

Ginny hummed as she finished adding ingredients to her teabag, then poured the already boiled water over it.

Tara shook her head. "I don't see how you can drink caffeine this late at night."

Ginny shrugged. "Never seems to bother me one way or the other," she admitted. "Can go without for weeks, then drink it all day, never notice a difference."

Ginny's slight British accent softened her words in an enchanting way, making Tara feel even less cool.

"But," Ginny added, "as lovely as the tea and company is, you have questions, I can tell."

"How can you tell?" Tara asked. She'd made a real effort to be polite and not just pounce on the other witch.

Ginny paused, considering. "There's an electric quality to the air. Charged, you know? No one else would notice it," she assured Tara. "It's just that our magics work well together, and so your impatience is spiking mine."

Tara nodded. That made sense. Their magics did work well together, combined without either of them willing it, making the little, day-to-day tasks easier.

Kyle still didn't trust it. He often questioned Tara when she unconsciously did magic, her wild magic taking care of her. And she still could see his point, that such power, unbridled, could lead her down the wrong path, making her arrogant.

As Ginny's tea steeped, Tara told Ginny about her vision that afternoon, of the coming storm. "I've never had a vision like that before," she said. "Not a waking dream. The Riprap man sent dreams to me when he was coming after me."

Ginny brought her finished tea over to the kitchen table where Tara was sitting. As she drew near, Tara felt their combined magic flare outwards.

None of Tara's flatmates would come into the kitchen now. Their magic had just seen to that, though neither Tara or Ginny had willed it. Tara wasn't even sure she knew how to make that happen, not without a sachet and a strong spell.

The natural magic was easier, and sometimes so much more powerful. Though it wasn't consistent. They had just as good of a chance that the magic would have flared and suddenly all of Tara's flatmates would be in the kitchen with them, drawn inexplicably there.

Ginny gave Tara a grin. "Seems we're here for a talk, then." She grew more serious. "Wind's my element," she said after a moment. "I can always follow it. It tugs me here or there."

Tara nodded. She'd come to realize that while getting to know the other witch better. Ginny had at least a dozen tamed winds who would go walking with her, though rarely all at the same time. They appeared as various breeds of dogs, from a huge mastiff to a tiny Pomeranian princess.

"The winds bring me news," Ginny said. "They've also told me of the huge amount of snow melting up river, and the coming storm."

"Really?" Tara asked, surprised.

"I did set them seeking, once I heard the news," she admitted. "But they confirmed what you and Richard have said. Now, your element is water, right?"

"Yes," Tara confirmed. She couldn't help but add, "I always feel at home there."

"But you haven't called a water spirit to you," Ginny said. "How else is the water to tell you what's coming if it doesn't have an easy way to talk with you? Other than to send you visions while you're surrounded by it?"

"Okay," Tara said slowly. "That kind of makes sense. Some water spirit brought me the vision. So that the water could protect me, right?"

"Eh, water's always tricksy," Ginny said. "Most of

the stories of merfolk and water spirits is all about them pretending to be helpful so that they can drown folk."

"So was the vision of the storm to get me to do something foolish?" Tara said, trying to puzzle out what the intention actually had been.

"Who knows?" Ginny said, shrugging her shoulders. "Maybe a bit of both. A warning of a coming trial, that ye may or may not survive."

Tarra thought about that for a moment. It sounded like just the sort of thing a water element might do. She remembered when she'd been walking the circle of water, and that in order to finish she'd needed to find balance. "What form does a water spirit take?" Tara asked after a few more moments.

"I don't know. I've never met a witch with a water familiar," Ginny said. "Or at least not as I know." She paused, then added with a grin, "Could be a horse."

Tara nearly snorted her tea out her nose. "Right. Where would I keep a horse? It couldn't just live in my bedroom, not like the other two." She couldn't help but grin at the idea of a tiny pony curled up on one side of the bed, with her in the middle, and Soot and Teruko on the other side. She'd have to get a bigger bed.

"They also appear as people," Ginny said. "At least according to legends and myths."

"I'll ask Richard to get me a list of the different forms a water spirit takes," Tara said.

"Then you'll try to call one to ye?" Ginny asked. The air between them suddenly sparked with excitement. "Tomorrow night?"

Tara took a deep breath. She hadn't thought about moving between the circles of the schooled witches for a while, not since her coven had turned their back on her. Kyle had been the one who passed her inward the last two times, first to the circle of air, then to the circle of fire where she now practiced.

But maybe she needed to move further inward, traverse another circle. Call a water spirit to her and bind it, so that she could face the river and the flood.

"Okay, I'll do it," Tara said. She hadn't been studying, but since water was her element, surely she natively knew enough to be able to do it?

"Yay!" Ginny said. She raised her tea mug in a toast. "Here's to taming another spirit."

Tara clinked her mug with Ginny's. Monday night was going to be fun.

~

GINNY AND TARA TALKED ABOUT WHAT THEY NEEDED to do in order to call a water spirit. Ginny reminded Tara that location was important. Tara had called Soot to her on the porch of Kyle's apartment. She'd called Teruko to her while standing beside a bonfire in the backyard of her new house. She needed to find someplace more neutral for calling the water spirit, so that she could get back to it easily. (Kyle might move from his condo someday, and she wasn't going to live in her current house forever.)

After they'd found a park that was close to Hallowed Ground, Tara sent an email to all the members of her coven, explaining what she wanted to try Monday night.

At least she had a long, restful sleep that night. She suspected that in part, it was due to being in Ginny's presence, her own magic calming as it meshed with Ginny's.

Tara spent Monday morning sitting on her bed, studying on her tablet with research books sprawled everywhere. Teruko complained that there wasn't enough space for him to lay down as well (even though he had the entire foot of the bed). So she had to shift the books around so the cat could curl up next to her thigh, sharing body heat.

At least Soot was probably outside playing somewhere and wasn't demanding her attention as well.

There wasn't enough time for Tara to memorize everything that she'd need to know for passing within, to the next circle. As a hedgewitch, she didn't need all this lore. As a schooled witch, she knew she'd fail the test because she didn't know all the uses all these herbs could be put to. She still intended on whizzing through the practicum.

Tara was just enough of a perfectionist that she really wanted to pass the lore part of any exam as well. Plus, she was learning useful things! She was going to have to start studying on a regular basis again.

When her phone rang, Tara took it as a welcome respite. "Hi, Kaede," Tara said happily, laying her book beside her.

Teruko opened one sleepy eye and glared at her for shifting her position.

"Hello, Tara," Kaede said. "How are you feeling this morning?"

"Rushed," Tara said honestly. "There's so much to study!"

"Cramming for the exam, eh?" Kaede said. "Good

thing you don't really need to pass one in order to call a water spirit."

"That's the truth," Tara said, feeling relieved and yet guilty at the same time. "So what's up?"

"I would like for you to reconsider your plans for this evening," Kaede said.

"Okay," Tara said, concerned. "Why?"

"I want you to call your water spirit here, in Hallowed Ground," Kaede said.

"Oh," Tara said. She hadn't been expecting that at all.

"I know, part of the reason why you wanted to be in a park was because it would be more easily accessed. I will give you my solemn vow that you'll always have access to Hallowed Ground," Kaede said.

"I don't want to invade your privacy," Tara said, shocked.

Kaede smiled at her. "You wouldn't be. We would conduct a spell together that would ensure you had access without disrupting me."

Tara nodded, thinking. "But what if the developer who owns the building sells it?"

Kaede gave a merry laugh. "I own the building. No one's about to sell it out from under me."

"Really? I didn't know that," Tara said. Though she didn't ask the question about where Kaede had gotten so much money, Kaede answered her anyway.

"Oni loaned me some of the money," Kaede said with a sigh.

Tara had learned that was the name of Kaede's grandmother, the elegant Japanese woman who came in every Saturday and Sunday and poured tea for the people who came there. It was her way of showing the people in the community respect. Even though they may or may not care for the tea, they needed to feel included that way. It was her own special magic, though Kaede claimed that Oni had no actual magic of her own.

"It's why Oni feels she can show up every weekend, as she claims the building is partly hers. I'm paying her off as quickly as I can, though," Kaede said.

Tara wasn't sure she wanted to know more about how the money worked for the charity, or how Kaede was getting more of it.

"How could a spirit enter the building though?" Tara asked. It was another reason why she'd wanted to work in a park and not at Hallowed Ground. The building was too protected.

"I'll crack open the spells for the evening," Kaede replied. "I was going to redo them during the spring solstice anyway. Remember?"

Tara nodded, then said, "Yes." The coven had been planning on meeting twice that week, on Monday for their usual circle, as well as on Wednesday to celebrate the solstice and redo the spells for Hallowed Ground. And possibly now call on the spirit of the harbor wall, though they might agree to meet on Tuesday to do that.

"Will the building still be safe?" Tara asked, concerned. "Before you put the spells back in place?"

"I didn't say I'd take them down, just crack them open a little," Kaede said, zir tone chiding. "Nothing else will get through."

Tara had to believe the other person. Kaede wouldn't do something rash or endanger zir community.

"All right," Tara said after a moment. As it was supposed to rain that night, it would certainly be nicer to hold the ceremony indoors. Though she'd been counting on the rain, to use it as part of her spell…

"I'll let you tell everyone the change of plans," Kaede said breezily. "Thank you," ze added.

"You're welcome," Tara said, swiping off the phone. She leaned against the headboard for her bed and thought for a moment, idly reaching out and petting Teruko's warm fur, getting rumbling purrs in return.

Would she have any problems calling the water spirit in the community center? Did she have to be outside in order to do it? She was already concerned about doing it in front of a large group of people, even though they were all part of her coven.

She'd have to bring a large bowl to contain the water she'd need, as the other times she called a spirit she'd already had some of that element nearby.

She sighed and told herself that it was all going to be okay. Water was her element. She could do this.

Normally, when Richard wanted to gain entrance to Hallowed Ground, he texted when he was just outside the door. He was such a mundane that Kaede's protection spells had him doubting that it was even the right building.

So Tara couldn't contain her surprise when Richard opened the front door and poked his head in. "Good," he said when he caught sight of Tara.

"How did you do that?" Tara asked, coming over to where he gingerly took off his soaking raincoat and shook off some of the excess rain outside the door.

"Took all my courage," Richard said. He gave a

huge sigh. "Still got butterflies, you know? But I did it."
He gave her a big smile.

"Richard the lion hearted," Tara teased him.

"Damn straight," he replied.

It took Tara another couple of moments to realize
that Richard's supposed ease and happiness was just a
mask. He was broken and crying inside.

"Oh, dear," Tara said.

He stopped her from hugging him. "Don't," he said,
his word clipped. "Or I'll just break down again."

Tara felt a lump form in her own throat. "Still
fighting?" she guessed.

"I'm losing her," Richard said, carefully studying
the floor. "I don't think she'll ever forgive me, or be
able to fully trust me after this."

"I'm so sorry," Tara said. And she was. "Let me
know if there's anything I can do to help, that the coven
can do." She felt guilty about Jeannie walking away,
though it wasn't necessarily her fault, not directly.

"Yeah," Richard said. He gave an audible gulp, then
looked back up at her, his mask firmly back in place.
"So we're calling a water spirit tonight, eh?" he said
giving her a determined smile.

"We are," Tara said, taking the hint to not ask him
any more about Jeannie or his relationship. "I'm just
about finished drawing the pentagram."

"Is there anything I can do?" Richard asked as he
did every time.

"Not with this, no," Tara said. "Tell me if you've
found out anything new about water spirits," she asked
instead.

"Lots of cultures had water spirits," Richard said,
falling easily into research librarian mode. He certainly

looked nerdy enough, in his huge black-rimmed glassed, his old blue jeans, and a red T-shirt that proclaimed that it was actually blue if you approached it fast enough.

"Most of the time, a water spirit either appears in the form of a person, or has another shape and can also take the form of a person. There are a few exceptions," Richard said, nodding to Kaede as ze came into the room. "There are water dragons, in Chinese myth. Though those usually either represent the sea, or thunderstorms. Mesoamerican myth is more concerned with rain than with sacred waters or streams. The Chaac usually have a human body with fish scales, and a snake-like head."

"That would be cool," Kaede offered. "If your water spirit manifested as a snake."

"At least that's a pet that I could easily keep," Tara said as she finished drawing the last line of the pentagram on the floor of the common room. "Instead of, say, a horse."

She'd drawn the pentagram in white chalk. Sitting in the center was a huge glass bowl with pretty flowers etched along the rim. It was full of pure water that Tara had blessed. She planned on using that as her water element.

Richard snorted, also seemingly amused by the idea of a horse manifesting.

"Did you loosen the protection spells for the building?" Tara asked, remembering that Richard had for the first time been able to get in without someone else opening the door first.

"I did," Kaede said. "Can you feel it?"

Tara extended her senses outward, seeking the perimeter of the building. It had always seemed so closed off to her, the space inside sacred, set apart from the mundane.

Now, instead of a hard border that protected the occupants, the wall had transmuted. It was still thick, but permeable.

"I think so," Tara said after a moment. "Still don't know how you do it."

Kaede smiled at her. "We all have our strengths," ze said.

Ginny was also able to enter the building without hesitation. Lucius had never noticed the barrier in the first place, as it had never been enough to hold back one of his kind. Kyle came in, his face quizzical, as if he had sensed the missing protections.

Normally, the group stood together in a circle, holding hands and sharing their magic.

Tonight, Tara had drawn out a protective pentagram in order to better focus the magic around her. Each of the other members of the coven would stand at their point of the star while she'd stand in the middle. It was the first time she'd done this, asked them to direct their magic to her instead of letting it flow around the circle. Kaede had agreed that this would probably be the best way for Tara to find her water spirit and bind it to her.

After everyone had taken their places, Tara stepped into the center of the pentagram. She heard Richard's gasp as the lines suddenly flared bright white.

Tara hadn't expected him to be able to see the magic, but she was glad that he could.

"Thank you for coming and being part of this calling tonight," Tara said solemnly. "I also thank the goddess Brigid for defending the earth. I thank the warrior Samil for defending its people," she said, continuing her prayer. She called on Hayvu to carry her words on the western winds to all the parts of the earth, and Eural to carry her words on the eastern winds. After also thanking Areebin, the protector of souls, Tara finally asked Bonana, the goddess of the water, to send one of her spirits forth.

Winds suddenly swirled through the large room, circling those standing at the points of the pentagram. Tara felt the wind tugging on her hair, which she'd worn down that night. She couldn't help but grin.

Now, Tara reached for the magic the others had generated. It wasn't as cohesive as when they were all connected in a circle. The edges were more diffuse, frayed by the growing wind. Instead of a magical mass, Tara had to reach for threads of magic, finding Lucius's strong cool line that tasted like wintergreen tea, then reached for Ginny's pepper-laced thread, then finally gathered together the others, pulling the power toward her.

She couldn't hold onto each thread individually, however. The easiest thing for her to do was to weave all that power together into a large golden net, as Kaede had done on more than one occasion when they threw their collected power upstairs, to heal the people sleeping above them.

While a net was easy, the back of her mind chittered at her. It wasn't the right shape, not for drawing in a water spirit. But she'd never thought of the form the magic would need to take for water, not specifically.

Tara continued on despite her misgivings. "I call on Juhali, spirit of the rain! I call on Onosh, spirit of the ocean! I call on the water spirits of the Columbia and

Willamette! Come. Bring me a piece of you, that I might better know your will!"

The sound of falling rain filled the room, a quiet, comforting spattering. Tara's skin didn't get wet, however, and she couldn't actually see the drops. The winds died down, as if the rain was hushing them, dampening their power.

Suddenly, the bowl of water sitting at Tara's feet lit up, as if a spotlight had hit it. White mist began rising out of it.

Tara tried to see what form the water spirit was taking. However, the form was shapeless at first, looking like billowing fog as it grew.

The golden net that Tara had gathered grew stronger between her hands. She raised her arms up above her head, then threw the net over the top of the mist.

The net passed through the mist and landed with a splashing sound on the floor, spreading out across the rest of the pentagram until it touched the toes of the rest of the coven.

Tara frowned. She'd suspected something was wrong with the net, that it wasn't the right shape to draw a water spirit to her. She didn't have time, though, to refocus and reform the magic flowing around her.

The white mist rising from the bowl was as tall as Tara now, and began to coalesce into a human-like figure. She couldn't tell if it was male or female.

Before the form took its full shape, it drew one foot up out of the water.

Tara caught her breath. Was it about to step out, onto the ground and come to meet her? She started humming a hymn of praise and welcome.

The figure kept raising its leg up, drawing the knee up to its waist.

However, instead of stepping out of the bowl, it stomped down with its foot.

The glass bowl shattered with a loud crack. Slivers of glass flew everywhere. Tara felt the sting of the shards striking her face and her bare hands. She took a step back, accidently smudging the pentagram and breaking the circle of power.

Water sloshed everywhere, much more flowing out of the bowl than what it had contained. The tops of Tara's shoes were suddenly soaked. At first, the water raced along the lines of the net that Tara had dropped. Then it spread, seeking all the corners of the room. It moved quickly enough that small, four-inch waves formed on top of the water in all directions.

"Contain it!" Kaede shouted. "Before it attacks the building!"

Soot suddenly appeared, pushing back against the water, not letting it touch the southern wall that he guarded. Teruko helped as well, the warm corner he protected suddenly water free. Ginny brought in her dozen winds as well, pushing back the water from where it wanted to creep.

Lucius clapped his hands. A loud crack of thunder followed. Water sizzled in the direction he glared, drying up instantly.

But it was too late. The wild water had soaked into the building, through cracks in the floor.

"I'm losing it," Kaede moaned. Zir face had grown pale. "The water is wrenching the building from my control."

"Join hands!" Tara commanded, racing over to stand beside Kaede. "Form a new circle!"

The coven gathered around quickly. Once they joined together, the magic surged in a strong pulse between them.

Before Tara could try to weave their magic into a coherent shape, Lucius had gathered all the threads together, pushing the newly joined power toward Kaede.

All of Tara's strength was suddenly drained from her. She tried not to fight it, though she could tell her magic wanted to resist. She wasn't an earth person, but a water person. Opposing the water was difficult.

Instead, Tara tried to focus on what Kaede was doing, how ze was shoring up the protection spells for the building. Zir spells went deep under the foundation, as if the building itself had roots that went through the earth, past the compacted dirt and down into the bedrock, resting on the stones there.

No wonder the building always felt so protected, the barriers so strong! Kaede didn't depend on the brick walls themselves for her spells.

Tara tried to ride along with the others and pass the wave of magic to Kaede, for her to bolster the roots. She still felt as though only half of her power was able to be tapped, the rest still fighting her, wanting to reach out to the water instead that rested just a little bit beyond the rock.

Finally, after a timeless time, Lucius narrowed the pull of power from each of them, like he was slowly closing off a spigot. The world blinked back to life.

Tara found herself swaying where she stood. Kyle collapsed to the floor as soon as she released his hand. Richard as well. Ginny stood with a dazed look on her face, probably identical to the one that Tara had on hers. Only Lucius and Kaede didn't seem diminished by the amount of magic they'd just passed.

"What…what happened?" Tara asked as she knelt beside Richard, checking to make sure he was okay. His eyes were open and glassy, but he nodded at her and mouthed the words, "I'm okay."

Kyle had pushed himself up to sitting, his head hanging down between his drawn up knees. "That was intense," he said softly.

Tara was worried about how he started to tremble.

"The water was trying to break down the building," Kaede said after a moment. "Tried to get into the walls and the floors. They're too structured. The water didn't want to be contained." Ze sighed. "I'm sorry, Tara. I shouldn't have suggested that you call a water spirit here. I hadn't realized how…formless water can be."

Tara gulped and nodded. "Neither had I." She herself was more of a structured person. And yet, water was her element.

Kyle looked up from where he was seated, glaring at both of them. "How much research did you do before you called us all here?" he said, the smooth-jazz tone of his voice buzzed off and jagged.

"There wasn't much she could research," Ginny said hotly. "What works for ye schooled witches isn't the same for us."

Tara nodded. "I did some," she admitted. "But there wasn't time to do a lot."

Kaede spoke up. "You're going to need to do a lot more. And soon." Ze grimaced. "That water is still mixed in the roots of this building. When the next rain comes, it will start eroding the foundation. If there's a big flood, the building will collapse."

Tara sighed, the weight of the problem landing hard on her shoulders. Though Soot and Teruko came up and offered comfort, she knew there was little they could do to help.

She had to figure out how to tame a water spirit so she could draw the water out from Hallowed Ground. And quickly. Before the promised rains came.

CHAPTER 4

Finding one of these traveler creatures has been more difficult than I initially believed. They are rare and skittish. However, I think I have developed the perfect trap. I had originally been haunting the rail stations, looking for travelers heading back east. A long journey isn't what these travelers are seeking, though. They go short distances, explore, then take another quick hop. I've moved my gaze from the railroad to the river. Short boat trips north of the city have appeared to capture the interest of more than one traveler. The next one will be epic, the boat overturning as it runs into an unexpected sandbar. And I will capture and use the souls of all those who perish in Mulinohana's waters.

Wilson Evermore, architect of the harbor wall and protector of Portland, 1928.

TARA BLINKED SLEEPILY AT THE TEXT SHE RECEIVED from Kyle the next morning when she finally got up around nine thirty.

Breakfast?

The text seemed innocent enough. But Tara had the impression that Kyle was still angry with her over her failed attempt to call a water spirit. He must have taken the day off, though, if he was asking about going out with her.

The coven was meeting again that evening, though not at Hallowed Ground. Instead, they were meeting at the harbor wall. They were going to try to engage with the spirit tied to the wall. Lucius insisted that while it wasn't a witch, it wasn't necessarily one of his kind either. But still a being of power, just someone…different.

Tara wasn't sure why he was so insistent that they try talking to the creature first. What sorts of insights could the being give them? He wanted to learn more about the construction of the harbor wall first hand, and the soul tied to the wall was their best bet. But Tara hadn't been able to come up with a different plan. The rains were coming. Chances were the harbor wall would fail. Soon.

They needed to do something.

Tara looked again at the text on her phone. She knew she couldn't come up with some lie about not receiving Kyle's text. She wouldn't feel good about doing that. Plus, she'd never be able to hide the fact from him, not when they'd be sharing magic again that night.

So Tara texted back that she'd only just gotten up (which was true) so could they do a late breakfast?

Pick you up at 11?

Tara knew there was no escaping, so she said sure before she tottered off for a hot shower and a long think. However, her brain wasn't cooperating that morning. She found herself staring off into space after she'd made a morning concoction of a bright green tea with chili flakes, rose hips, ginger, then added some lavender and vanilla to smooth it out.

Tara sat in the middle of her bed staring out at nothing. She had books to study. Herbs to review. Richard had sent her even more information about water spirits and myths. But her body was so tired. Listless. As if the water inside of her had grown muddy and dull.

She'd never felt this bad when she'd been fighting the Riprap man. Never this exhausted. What had happened? What had tapped her magic so hard? Had it been Lucius the night before?

No, that wasn't it. Or rather, that was only partially it.

Her magical self had been fighting the strengthening spells that Kaede had been trying to erect. It went against her watery nature to be so confined.

Yet, Tara was going to have to help on Wednesday night, when Kaede tried to rebuild all her protection spells again. She wasn't sure how, though, to balance the two sides of her nature.

Tara had moved her musings to the street corner by the time Kyle showed up. It was nice to have a friend who had a vehicle that morning. She wasn't sure she could face either a bus or the MAX.

Kyle still drove a chocolate brown Mini Cooper. It took an effort for Tara to fold herself into the seat as always. However, the cooper had more than enough headroom for both of them.

"Took the day off?" Tara asked Kyle, as he was dressed in light green sweater that looked amazing against his black skin instead of his one of his fancy suits.

"I have so many sick days piled up it isn't funny," Kyle told her with a grin. "I'm getting to the stage of 'use them or lose them' though. So I figured breakfast would be a good idea today."

"I'm glad you called me," Tara said, mostly truthfully. She did in fact miss her old friend. They still had regular movie nights where they'd sit and watch bad 1970s TV and giggle. But they weren't as close as they'd once been, not when they'd been living together. Plus, Tara was so busy all the time now.

Kyle drove them to a neighborhood dive, "J's Breakfast." It was an incredibly popular restaurant during the weekend, with a line out the door and up the block. However, on a Tuesday, mid-morning, it was relatively empty.

J's was one of the skinniest restaurants Tara had ever been in. Just inside the door to the right ran a long bar, all the way to the back of the restaurant, with a dozen padded stools that swiveled attached to the floor in front of it. And that was it. There was no room for extra tables. On the other side of the wall behind the bar ran the long kitchen. At the end of the bar was a single multiuse bathroom, as well as a door leading out to the alley out back that was frequently open, carrying the scent of eggs, waffles, bacon, and rich coffee out to the neighborhood.

The Formica of the countertop had been replaced

sometime in the last few years, as it was still mostly smooth and gray, not stained and cracked like the older version had been. Some of the pads on the stools had been replaced as well so they were no longer split and cracked, the padding falling out, or held together with duct tape. But that was all that had changed in J's since the place had opened back in the 1930s.

Behind the stools, the cheap '70s paneling was covered with framed photographs of parties held at the restaurant through the years, including the suits of the '40s and the wildly colorful kaftans of the '80s.

Tara surprised Kyle by ordering coffee as well, though she asked for merely half a cup and a boatload of cream.

"What?" she asked in her defense when the two large mugs were plunked down in front of them. "I need the caffeine," she explained after dosing the coffee with cream and pouring a steady drizzle of sugar into the cup.

Kyle nodded. "I get that," he said.

They both ordered omelets. Now it was her turn to be surprised, as Kyle ordered the garden omelet.

"What?" he said, deliberately teasing her. "If I didn't get it, you'd start pointing out how I wasn't eating enough vegetables."

Tara had to acknowledge the truth in that. They talked of recent news, not of magic, covens, or floods. Tara felt herself relaxing despite the extra caffeine. She really had missed her old friend.

Finally, after Kyle had insisted on paying for breakfast, they both got extra coffee in to-go cups and decided to take a nice walk through the neighborhood. It would be another day or so before the clouds blew in, and the March sunshine was warm and inviting.

As soon as Tara stepped out of the restaurant, Soot appeared at her side.

"Everything okay?" Kyle asked as Tara paused to spend a moment petting Soot's head.

Tara wasn't about to admit that Soot had picked up Tara's worry about Kyle. "Yeah," she said after a moment. "Just checking in on me."

"Good," Kyle said. He grimaced. "I wouldn't have to want to try to defend myself from him."

Tara opened her mouth then shut it again. Kyle wasn't wrong that Soot would attack him if he tried to hurt her.

But Kyle wasn't about to attack her, was he?

They slowly made their way down the street, pausing to look at the many windows of the ma and pa shops that still occupied most of the storefronts. The bookstore didn't interest Tara, as it was mostly computer and technical books, but one of the shops had cute nautically themed T-shirts for sale, and she really liked the octopus one where the tentacles were dissolving into numbers and magical symbols.

"So I know that you didn't take me out to breakfast just for my scintillating conversation," Tara said as they reached the corner and turned up the quiet side street, away from the traffic and other pedestrians.

Kyle grimaced. "I'm worried about you. You did ask me to play your good conscience, you know."

"I know," Tara said, nodding. "So what would my conscience say to me this morning?"

"That you need to watch yourself so that you don't fall into the trap of being arrogant," Kyle said bluntly.

"I...what?" Tara said after a moment.

"You didn't know how to call a water spirit," Kyle

said. "Not really. You just figured you could wing it as water is your element."

Tara bent her head, acknowledging her guilt. She really hadn't spent the time she needed meditating on the form, not like she had before she'd called Teruko.

"I know you're a hedgewitch as well as a schooled witch. But you should have been better prepared."

"You're right," Tara said quietly. She really should have taken more time and been better prepared.

"There are still things you can learn from the lore," Kyle insisted. "If you'd studied more, you would have learned about sachets that could have been placed in the corners of the building, to protect it from the water or floods."

Tara sighed. Kyle was speaking the truth. She shouldn't have just assumed that she knew enough to call a water spirit. She remembered the time when she'd tried to walk the circles, to pass inward to the circle of air. How Aaloka, her former mentor and teacher, had pushed her even when Tara hadn't felt ready.

Aaloka had told Tara that she was ready, and was standing in her own way.

This time, Tara really hadn't been ready.

"I admit that I fucked up," Tara said. "And you're right, I was starting to get arrogant. Instead of studying and preparing, I thought the spirit would just come to me, as water is my element." She took a sip of her overly sweet coffee, the sugar tasting bitter now.

Kyle nodded and looked relieved. "Good. I'm glad I don't have to be more of an asshole this morning."

Tara gave him a reassuring smile. "Sometimes, it's necessary for even my friends to be assholes and tell me where I've screwed up." Then Tara took a deep breath.

"The question is, what do I do now? I don't have a lot of time to study, to prepare. But I have to be able to call a water spirit to me. And soon. So I can help repair the damage the first one did—is doing—to Hallowed Ground."

"Do you?" Kyle asked, raising one eyebrow in her direction. "Don't you think that Kaede can handle it zirself?"

Tara heard the underlying question that Kyle was really asking: was she just being arrogant again, assuming that she had to fix the problem?

"Water isn't Kaede's element," Tara said slowly. "Earth is. You know ze's a fifth level witch, right?"

Kyle nodded. "I did know. I still don't know where ze studied, however." He sounded frustrated. "I've asked around, but I can't find a coven that once admitted zir."

"Ze talks about zir grandmother ensuring that ze started studying magic at a young age," Tara commented. "Perhaps it wasn't a formal coven, but just friends and relatives."

"That would make sense. But again, back to the original question. Do you need to help Kaede fix the protection spells?" Kyle said.

Tara wanted to point out that the entire coven would be helping Kaede fix the spells on the equinox. However, that wasn't really what he was asking about.

"I do need to have a better understanding of water and water spirits if I'm to help zir exorcize the one that's in the building's roots now," Tara said. She nodded, the words and images coming to her as she thought about it. "The water is trying to break the earth free. We don't need to capture it, though, or draw it out. Instead, water will always take the path of least resistance. We just need to provide it a hole it can flow down into."

"Huh," Kyle said, nodding. "That makes sense. But you're still going to have to nudge it along that path."

"And that's what I need to study," Tara said. "How to entice the water to follow me."

Soot had been a puppy, and had eagerly wanted to join with her, be a part of her life. He hadn't been lonely as a wind, not exactly. But he'd been willing to be tamed.

Teruko had taken a lot of coaxing to bring him out of the flames. Then again, Tara had studied fire more, and had been able to talk of the hidden gods, worshipped by the fire itself, the ones that had no human names. That she'd had the knowledge of those had at least gotten Teruko to listen to her. That, and the fact that Tara still always carried a spark of warmth within her.

The water though…it was just a part of her. She didn't know how to draw more of it to her.

"With both Soot and Teruko, you had a specific source of that element," Kyle said.

Tara shrugged. "I had that bowl of water. Look how well that turned out." She sighed. "Ginny did say that water was always tricksy. That it would both try to protect me at the exact same time it would try to drown me."

"Lovely," Kyle said. "Are you sure you even want a water spirit as a familiar?"

Tara gave a choked laugh. "Yeah, I do." She paused, considering. "It isn't arrogance," she assured Kyle. "It's honestly the next step. It's the next part of my journey. It's where I have to go from here, or die trying."

Kyle sighed, obviously not believing her. "But why?" he asked again.

"I just do," Tara said. She wasn't being obstinate. It was the right thing for her to do.

Kyle still made a face. "I still consider you my best friend," he said after a few moments of tense silence. "But we're just going to have to agree to disagree about this one."

"All right," Tara said. A small lump formed in her throat.

She'd known that this day was coming. Kyle was a schooled witch. He didn't understand Tara's hedgewitch powers. And she was never going to be able to explain them to him.

Hopefully, however, they had enough other things connecting them that he wouldn't leave the coven.

~

TARA SPENT THE REST OF THE AFTERNOON CRAMMING, as it were, studying all the herbs she needed to learn for the next level if she was passing within, like a schooled witch. Her eyes hurt. She squeezed them tightly together, pressing her palms against them, trying to bring more moisture back to them as the shadows grew longer.

Finally, though, Tara put the books to the side of her bed. She reached forward, stretching to grab her ankles and stretch out her back.

Teruko hopped onto the bed at that moment. "Mrrr?" he trilled as he head-butted her leg.

"Fine, yes," Tara told him, skritching him under the

chin. "I know. It's awful. I haven't been paying any attention to you at all all afternoon."

Teruko stopped rubbing his head all along her leg and looked up at her, his golden and blue eyes staring hard at her.

"What?" Tara asked. Obviously the spirit wanted to tell her something. "I had to study before I called you, too," she told him.

The cat tilted his head to one side, still observing her. If she was to guess, she would say that he had a contemplative look on his face and was thinking deep philosophical thoughts.

Or he was just considering the best way to get her to pay more attention.

Teruko very deliberately turned his head and licked the side of her hand. Instead of a raspy tongue, a trail of fire raced across Tara's skin.

"Ouch!" Tara said, jerking her hand away, drawing it up to her chest. "What did you do that for?"

Teruko jumped from the bed and stalked away, disappearing before he reached the door.

Obviously, the cat believed that Tara was doing something wrong. But what? Or was he just pissy because she was studying an element that wasn't his?

She wasn't sure what had upset him. But she knew better than to try to call the cat back. He would spitefully ignore her, probably for the next week or so.

With a sigh, Tara reached for her books again. But she didn't want to study anymore. Her head felt full of mush. Instead, she picked her books up, lightly put them on the floor beside the bed, set an alarm on her phone, and curled up for a quick nap.

TARA DREAMED OF WALKING IN WHAT LOOKED TO HER like an English garden. While there were wild roses growing along the edges of it, and ivy taking over the wall, the grass had been trimmed to within an inch of its life. All the flowers were in their beds, the daffodils separate from the crocuses, which were separate from the bluebells and the lilies of the valley. Nothing was out of place. Artistically laid out rocks formed a spiraling path through the area.

Tara found she couldn't step off the gravel walkway, that instead, she could merely walk the tamed roads. It frustrated her. The path never led close enough to the roses. Their scent tantalized her. She could hear them whispering on the slight breeze. She had to get to them, but she didn't know how.

Around and around the garden Tara walked. It was worse than the meditation maze she'd walked when passing within. She was so close to her target, only to be led away with the next few steps. She stopped and leaned over to get closer to the roses, maybe even bend over enough to touch a branch. As soon as she reached for one, though, the winds sprang up and pushed the roses back.

The winds also tried to force Tara from her path. But she knew, in that perfect logic of dreams, that as soon as she deviated from the rock walkway, the greenery would eat her alive.

Long afternoon shadows stalked across the green lawn. The air grew chilly. The delightful scent of the roses was now mingled with decay. Tara wasn't going to be able to capture her rose before it had stopped blooming.

Finally, unable to take it any longer, Tara forced herself to step off the path.

The grass tickled her now bare feet, soft and springing on top with good, solid dirt underneath, cool and carrying its own earthy scent.

But the grass grew more spongy. The roses against the wall seemed to retreat. Though Tara had stepped off the path at where she'd been closest to the rose trees, there was now an entire field between her and her prize.

She made the mistake of starting to run.

The grass no longer grew on solid earth, but floating on a pond.

Tara quickly sunk knee deep in the waters. Her feet slipped against the slimy mud. Then the ground tried to catch hold of her, sucking at her toes, making it more difficult with each step.

She couldn't go backwards. An endless ocean splayed out behind her.

She could only go forward, toward that distant shore, even though the water was rising and she was sure to drown.

For the first time, Tara felt afraid of the water. She tried to bluster through it. Water was her element. She shouldn't be afraid. She could swim out.

But she knew she couldn't. The roots of the grass would form a net and hold her, while the water would slip through.

Night was coming quickly. She had to get out.

Water was all about a balance, finding the point between raging and trickling.

Tara woke up still floundering. She sat up in her bed,

panting. Though she coughed, no water came up out of her lungs. She still felt waterlogged.

The fiery path across her hand that Teruko had licked suddenly came back to her.

Obviously the cat had been trying to tell her something, something about her own very nature.

But what?

~

THE BUS LET TARA OUT A FEW BLOCKS AWAY FROM where the coven was meeting. They'd found a park midway along the harbor wall. Though there were no clouds, the air had stayed warm. Tara knew it was the start of the pineapple express winds blowing their way, sure to dump several inches of warm rain on them starting tomorrow.

Even with the dim light, Tara could tell this wasn't the best neighborhood. Tags covered the garbage cans on the corner. Graffiti murals were painted across the fronts of the garages. At one point this neighborhood had probably been cute, but it had gone to seed. The sidewalks were cracked.

An encampment of homeless stretched along the driveway of an abandoned house. Tara would have to remember to come back and talk with them, to let them know that the area might be flooding tomorrow and that they were directly in the path of the water.

They wouldn't necessarily believe her, of course.

And their deaths really would be her fault, as the Riprap man was sure to claim.

Tara hurried along, drawn toward the light she saw just down the street. Lucius had prepared the area for them. The light that Tara saw came from the top of his cane that he held aloft like a torch. Anyone outside of their coven would be repelled by the light.

Lucius wore his usual impeccable black coat, though he'd added knee-high black leather boots that evening. They had a square toe and looked much more solid than Tara's own short waterproof boots.

"I'm glad you're here first," Lucius said, nodding to Tara. His silver hair gleamed in the light he held, though his normally blue eyes appeared black. "I wouldn't presume to give you advice—"

"Yes, you would," Tara snapped at him.

His eyebrows raised up at her.

"I'm sorry," Tara said. "I'm just tired. And I don't know what to do. How to stop this flood from coming."

Lucius nodded. "I see," he said.

"You wouldn't presume to give me advice…" Tara prompted him after he'd been quiet for a while.

"True," Lucius said. He sighed, and seemed to come to a decision. "You need to decide what is right for you," he said after a moment. "Just think about it."

"What do you mean?" Tara asked, confused.

"Part of the issue with you humans is that you're always racing off to do something or another," Lucius said, "instead of thinking about it. Forming a plan. Perhaps considering the consequences or even what the correct path is."

Tara forced her hands to unclench, though she really felt as though she wanted to slap Lucius and his smug attitude from his handsome face. "I've been doing trying to do that," she said, her jaw clenched so she wouldn't scream. "I've been studying. Thinking."

"Ah, there's your problem," Lucius said. "You need

to be meditating and feeling deeply. You're a witch. That means seeking the answers within, not without."

Tara nearly growled. Hadn't that been how she'd gotten into trouble in the first place?

"Meditate on it," Lucius said, though the words sounded more like a command. "Don't just grasp at the first solution that comes to hand."

"I don't have time," Tara pointed out.

"Make the time," Lucius said. His human mask slipped a little.

Tara felt a shiver of fear run through her. She refused to take a step backwards, away from this being, though the power flowing off him buffeted against her skin like harsh waves.

"How? How do I make the time?" Tara asked. She found her hands balled up in tight fists and didn't bother releasing them.

"Go deep," Lucius said. He seemed amused by her aggression. "Think deeply." He looked past her. "Ah, Kaede. Welcome."

Tara couldn't help the anger that still radiated off her. She was trying, damn it! Trying to learn enough. To be enough. To do enough so that she wouldn't lose thousands of lives.

How could going deep help her? She'd drown if she went deep. She couldn't pass through the water as she had passed through the fire. She couldn't live and die as she had with the old tree. She had to do something else with the water, find that balance.

And soon.

❧

THEY STOOD IN A CIRCLE, HOLDING HANDS BESIDE THE river. Though Lucius had killed the light from this cane, he still generated a soft glow so they weren't standing in complete darkness.

The sound of the rushing water soothed Tara's nerves, as did the smell of the wet grass. It was too early to hear crickets or frogs, but they'd start their singing soon. She held hands with Ginny on one side, and just held pinky fingers with Kyle on the other.

They stood in a different order tonight, the one that Lucius had put them in instead of the order they normally stood in. There was no doubt, though, that Lucius was the center of the circle, despite how he stood beside them, joined physically with the rest of them.

Tara still led the group in their initial prayers, starting this time with Bonana, the goddess of the waters before thanking the fires by their unknowable names, the earth underneath their feet and the winds. Only at the very end did she make a mention of the defenders of the people and the guardian of souls.

It just seemed to her that the elements were more important that night, rather than the other spirits.

Lucius took up the prayer next. He thanked gods and goddess who Tara didn't know, the names rolling off his tongue. His voice would have graced any chapel, the deep tones ringing solemnly through the air. He actually sounded sincere, and not sarcastic for once.

She should have realized that of course, Lucius and his kind had their own gods and goddesses, though she didn't really see Lucius as someone who would spend a lot of time being grateful or in prayers.

Tara added her magic to the threads being gathered. It felt easier this time, as though her magic wasn't fighting against her. Then again, it also felt as if she pushed her magic along, instead of having it pulled from her.

Lucius formed a bubble of magic around them. It felt vaguely familiar to Tara. It took a moment for her to remember her dream, where she'd been trying to hold back the wave on the river. She'd formed a similar sort of bubble shield around her.

Huh. So it was actually a thing? Not just something her imagination had come up with?

Then again, Tara knew she wasn't the most imaginative person in the world. She tended to be very practical and not fanciful.

She was going to have to remember to ask Lucius about this spell later, to see if it was possible for her waking self to make something similar.

Then Tara's stomach lurched. Sour bile rose up and she swallowed hard to get rid of it.

The group had started to sink beneath the ground. The last time she'd done this had been using Miss Lucy's potion, and her stomach still associated the two.

Tara looked across the circle to Richard, whose eyes were so wide they appeared to be popping out of his head. She tried to send reassurance to him as the ground rose up, the cool earth now the level of her knees. At least he didn't look as though he'd bolt and break the circle. Probably his fear, as well as his curiosity, held him in place.

Down they went, starting off slowly then rocketing, like a high-speed elevator. The cold quickly sank into Tara's bones. She tried to call up the spark of fire that lived deep within her but it was sluggish in response.

It, too, was still tired.

When Tara had visited the witch at the base of the Morrison bridge, she'd landed in what looked like living room carved out of the rock, with a cold fireplace despite the bright blue flames and solid rock walls.

Or as the witch had called it, "Cell sweet cell."

The group landed in a vaguely round chamber. This wasn't someone's home. The walls were plain rock and soft dirt lay under their feet. It looked like a cave, with several tunnels branching off of it. The rock gave off a strange white glow, as though living mist covered it. A slight breeze blew around them, tugging at Tara's hair and carrying the scent of dust and ancient dirt.

Before anyone could ask if this was the right place, a figure came out of one of the tunnels.

She was taller than Tara, over six feet. Long silver-white hair flowed straight down from her center part, ending close to her waist. Her skin had the same pale glow as the rock, as did her clothing—a loose pair of trousers with a long-sleeved shirt hanging over it, belted at the middle. Her bare feet seemed out of place. Tara would have expected solid boots.

Though Lucius still physically stood with the rest of them in the circle, what appeared to be an avatar of the being pulled away, turning to face the woman. His avatar took on that same whitish glow as the other spirit.

Neither of them were ghosts. Though they had the same glowy white coloration as a ghost, she couldn't see through them. Ghosts were always transparent. This was a spirit form that she'd not heard of before. Could witches do it? Or was this just an ability of beings of power?

Or was her spirit form more colorful, as she had traveled without her body before.

The wind whistled more loudly through the chamber. Tara also thought she heard the sound of rain pattering around her. The smell of the river suddenly loomed, full of wet moss and decay.

"You have come," the woman whispered. The wind suddenly died down. "As promised."

Lucius pulled himself more stiffly upright at that. "I didn't promise anything."

"Ah, no, not you. The other. Who first took my soul," the woman said, swaying. "The Riprap man."

A spike of fear ran through Tara. That didn't forebode anything good.

A sigh filled the chamber. The sound of rain increased.

"I just have to wait until the rains come, now," the woman said. "And I will be free."

Tara didn't understand what was happening. Mist sprang from the walls, blocking her view of the two spirits.

Ginny called up a quick wind to clear the way.

The woman now had her hands on Lucius's shoulders. His spirit form stood frozen in place.

Tara gasped when she realized that his boots were dissolving. She knew that once his bare feet touched ground, he'd be stuck here forever.

The spirit would change places with him. He would stay here and she would be free.

"Up!" Tara commanded. "Back above the earth!"

Tara thrust Lucius to the side, drawing the focus of power to herself. Kaede wove the rest of them together into a single unit. Tara could tell that ze had some difficulty with Lucius, who now stood there like a dead weight.

Fortunately, Tara had experience with this sort of travel and had a good feel of where her physical body still stood in the circle above the ground. She grabbed onto the threads of her soul, still planted in her body, and *pulled*, trying to lift the entire group back up above ground.

It was slow going at first. Tara's metaphorical arms ached and shook as she tugged at the threads above her. The bubble enclosing the group felt too heavy. She couldn't drag such a large structure with all these souls up. She wasn't strong enough.

Then Kyle's strength flowed into her, giving her the power to start to lift them.

Once the group was no longer touching the ground of the chamber, Tara was able to lift them much more quickly through the earth. It wasn't a high-speed elevator this time, though. More like an old fashioned clunky one, that tended to get stuck between floors.

Tara couldn't split her attention, couldn't look over at Lucius. She stayed focused on that thread up above, pulling her up. She had to get them all safe.

The sound of water buoyed her spirits and renewed her determination. She could follow the sound of the river. The others were hearing it too, whether they realized it or not. That made lifting the bubble of magic so much easier as it wasn't merely her senses drawing them up.

Finally, they popped up above the earth. Tara settled easily into her body, stepping into her skin and breathing a sigh of relief.

She blinked and looked around at the others. They all stood with her, various expressions of shock and relief on their faces. They still all held hands and were joined together in a circle.

Then the circle broke, their hands no longer joined.

Lucius fell to his knees, then over onto his side.

Kaede reached him first, though Kyle was right beside zir.

Even in the dim light, Tara could tell that Lucius had grown incredibly pale. Almost as white as his spirit form.

Finally his eyes blinked open. "It was a trap," he said, his normally smooth voice grating and harsh. "Eunida—she stole…she stole as much of my power as she could," he added.

Tara looked around at the others. She had no idea what that meant. No one else seemed to have a clue either.

Lucius closed his eyes and took a deep breath before continuing. "It means that now, when the rains come, Eunida can destroy the harbor wall when she escapes. Blow it to pieces." He coughed, his voice starting to return to normal. "Unless I take her place."

Tara couldn't help but gasp. "No," she said plainly. She wasn't about to let that happen.

Lucius chuckled. "Of course, that's a very noble reaction," he said, his tone returning to its normal sarcastic gait. "But are you sure that you wouldn't rather sacrifice one being for all the souls in Portland that you might save?"

"There has to be another way," Tara said. The others in the coven all nodded.

"But you forget, I'm not human," Lucius said. The mask slipped, whether on purpose or by accident, reminding Tara and the rest of just how alien this creature laying on the ground actually was.

Richard took a step back, visibly shaken. So did Ginny. Tara stood her ground, grinding her teeth together, as did Kyle and Kaede.

"I always said I'd be using you and expected the same in return," Lucius reminded her. "No hard feelings if I become the sacrificial goat."

"Do you want to be bound to the wall?" Kyle asked. He seemed choked up. Then again, Lucius had been his off and on lover.

"Of course not," Lucius said. "Don't be silly."

"Then we'll figure out something else," Tara said firmly. "We're not sacrificing you or anyone else."

Lucius merely chuckled at her pronouncement. "For now."

CHAPTER 5

Capturing Eunida proved more difficult than I'd ever imagined. Such power! And all of it willfully squandered on herself and her travels. She insists on creating her own prophesy, that another will come and take her place someday. She doesn't realize that it will be my doing when that occurs, that I will replace her, releasing her soul to the ever after, or to Hell, or to wherever such beings go. Her soul will protect the entire length of the harbor wall, however, for as long as it lasts. And the river will be cleaner, too, sewers no longer dumping their contents into the water. At least not these, though there are others up and down the riverbank that continue to do damage. One day, perhaps mankind will awaken to the danger of polluting their own nests.

Wilson Evermore, Spirit Tamer and Clean Water Evangelist, 1929

TARA WOKE FEELING RESTLESS. WHEN SHE'D GOTTEN home, she'd tried going deep as Lucius had insisted, but she'd just ended up falling asleep. She sat up in her bed, trying to remember her dreams in case they had any hints or clues about what to do, but nothing brilliant came to her.

She couldn't help but groan when she saw an envelope had been pushed under her doorway. Who else had died? Whose death would the Riprap man blame her for this time?

She delayed getting up for a few more moments, checking her phone for messages. Kyle had taken Lucius home from the park and had promised to look after him for the day. Richard was going to do more research to see if he could find either Eunida or a myth that covered her type of being. According to Lucius, she wasn't one of his kind, but something called a traveler.

No important messages or emails. With a sigh, Tara got up, wrapped herself in her robe, and shuffled over to the door.

While the envelope was the same, instead of being a clipping about a death, it was about the failing of a dam just north of the city. Again, the words, "YOUR FAULT" were printed in red crayon.

Tara wasn't sure what the Riprap man was getting at. How could the fault at the dam be her fault? What did it matter?

Then she realized that the clipping was from that morning.

The dam had failed because too much water was pouring down from the mountains.

The chance of flooding in Portland had just gone up significantly.

And more rains were coming.

~

Despite the rain already pouring from the sky, Tara kept her promise to Mulinohana and spent the morning standing on one of the piers, throwing rose petals into the water.

Tara sang hymns to the water and the river, praising the coming rains as well as thanking the river for its bounty. Water dripped off the wide brim of her black rain hat and onto her bare hands. Her pretty purple waterproof boots were up to the task of the onslaught, as was her bright orange rain jacket. Her jeans, however, were soaking wet where they were exposed to the elements, from the top of her thighs to just below her knees.

However, Tara didn't call up the spark of fire that lived inside her to keep herself warm. Fire and water were fierce enemies. It felt disrespectful for her to call the fire while fulfilling her promise to the river spirit.

Tara sang and scattered pink and red rose petals across the water. The last time she'd done this, at the winter solstice, the water had sucked at the petals eagerly, pulling them under. Tara had taken it as a sign that her offering had been accepted.

This time, the petals stayed on the surface of the water, floating quickly downstream, as if Mulinohana really didn't like this offering.

Tara wasn't sure what to do, despite her misgivings. She finished her ritual, shaking the petals off her wet fingers then jamming her freezing cold hands into her pockets. Though the air felt warm, the rain was still cold. She stayed where she was, rocking back and forth on her feet, thinking.

The river flowed swiftly under the wooden pier, a dark, brown-gray color. Tara stared into the depths, trying to understand what the river was saying.

It didn't seem to care that she was there, fulfilling her promise. It had its own intent, to flow mighty and free. It resented everywhere man had interfered with its flow.

With a shock, Tara realized that the river itself was looking forward to flooding Portland.

But what about those places marked Sacred to You?

The Riprap man had sacrificed the witches in order for the bridges to be safe.

Would you break your Word?

Tara felt as though only part of the river acknowledged her claim. But the waters had divided, somewhere upstream. They'd swollen with so much snowmelt that the composition was no longer the same.

Mulinohana still existed, but his will had been diluted.

And the rest of the waters were angry.

Do not break your vow, Tara warned.

The waters didn't bother sneering at her. She wasn't important enough for that.

They were planning on running their course, no matter what the consequences.

❀

Tara called Richard as she walked toward Hallowed Ground. She was working there for the rest of the afternoon, would take a quick dinner break, then meet the rest of them. Normally she'd be teaching at the Y that afternoon, but she'd arranged to take the days off around the equinox months before.

"Tell me you have some good news," Tara begged as she slogged through the rain.

"According to the weather forecasters, the pineapple express won't start really dumping water on us until later tonight," Richard said. His voice sounded grim. "All the pieces are in place for a huge flood. The city has already put all of its emergency crews on high alert."

"Not sure that's good news," Tara said sourly.

"It means the city is taking the threat seriously," Richard said. "I do think that's good news. There's a chance fewer people will die because we're expecting the worst."

"No, they're not," Tara said. "They're expecting some sort of flooding. Not that the harbor wall will explode as a mythical creature blows up her prison, fed by the energy we gave her last night." She was still pissed that they'd fallen for such a trap.

Why had Lucius insisted that they go talk to Eunida? Or was it a fate that he hadn't been able to escape? Had Eunida been calling to him? Or was this something that the Riprap man had done?

"Was Lucius serious when he thought that you'd actually sacrifice him? To save the city?" Richard asked.

Tara sighed. "He was." She took a minute to shake her head, sending drops cascading down from her wide-brimmed rain hat. "He isn't human," she added after a few moments. "He'd do the same thing to one of us in a heartbeat."

Richard gave a low whistle. "That's what I thought. I'm starting to understand just what that means, though." He sighed and paused.

"What?" Tara asked. Obviously he wanted to say something else.

"Well, Jeannie has kind of been following along with the flooding and everything," Richard said slowly.

Tara rolled her eyes. She hadn't forbidden Richard from talking about what they'd been doing recently. Maybe he thought telling Jeannie about the coming flood would help. Or maybe he was just trying to warn her away, trying to save her.

"She said that if we can prevent the flooding, maybe she'll accept that witches can do something good," Richard said all in a rush. "I mean, no pressure or anything. Save a couple thousand people, millions of dollars in property damage, and my relationship all at the same time."

Tara had to chuckle, as Richard had intended her to. "I'll do my best," she promised.

"I know you will," Richard said. "You'll come up with something. You have magic, right?"

Tara shook her head. Magic couldn't solve everything. Otherwise, as Jeannie had pointed out, the world would be in much better shape, wouldn't it?

"I'll see you later tonight," Tara said. They were still going to try to shore up the defenses of Hallowed Ground.

Tara swiped off her phone and took a moment to zip it carefully into one of her jacket pockets, getting it out of the rain. Then she took a deep breath and turned the corner, seeing the building for the first time in a couple of days.

Curses bubbled up out of Tara. The building suddenly looked old. The bricks no longer seemed perfectly aligned. The second story sagged in the middle, as if the supports had suddenly weakened. Peeling white paint covered the window frames. The smell of rotting drywall seeped over Tara, as if mold now grew between the walls.

And that was what the building felt like from the outside.

Tara steeled herself as she approached the volunteer door in the back.

Wait, was that graffiti? It disappeared as soon as she approached it.

The building was vulnerable to all attacks now. Human and non-human.

As were the souls inside.

TARA KEPT LOOKING AROUND THE FRONT HALL. AS THE room felt so different she kept expecting for it to look different as well. Nothing had changed physically, though. The floor was still plain, scarred wood. The walls were decorated with drawings from the youngsters, as well as with government posters advising where people could get help, numbers for the homeless to call.

The same three rows of long tables were set up near where Tara had her "teashop." But no adult sat in the corner reading to the kids. Instead, the kids wandered with books in their hands, looking for someone to read to them. The activity corner was loud and crazy, and one child stood in the corner in time out, crying.

Soot and Teruko hadn't accompanied Tara that day, probably not wanting to face the chaos. Plus, only a few of the teens had asked for teas that afternoon.

If Tara had to put a name to the sour tang on the air, she'd call it hopelessness. This room used to be full of hope, of determination to be better, do better. Now, it was barely a refuge for those it sheltered.

It broke Tara's heart to see how the energy had flowed out of the room. She was determined to patch the building back up. Hopefully, just drawing the water out of the ground, purifying the spells there, would fix most of what had broken.

She wasn't sure it would be enough.

Was this why the Riprap man sacrificed a spirit at the base of new construction? So that his protection spells would last? Though he'd hunted and killed witches, probably needlessly, his intentions had always been good: he was there to protect the city of Portland.

Eric came up just as Tara was starting to load her canisters on the cart and take them back into the kitchen. "Hi," Tara said, trying to give him a big smile.

It mostly worked.

"Hi," he said, seemingly shy. He stood in front of her table, shifting from one foot to the other. His skin had that waxy look to it again, his eyes too big for his face. His black hair hung stringy down over his shoulders. He hunched over in his jacket, as if he couldn't get warm that afternoon. (Tara had had the same feeling, though she knew consciously that the room was the same temperature it had always been.)

"Is there something I can make for you?" Tara asked when Eric still didn't say anything after a few moments.

He looked up at her, his lips pressed so tightly together the skin around his mouth had gone stark white.

Tara waited. It was something she'd learned, having the patience to wait until one of the teens finally figured out what they wanted to say, not rushing them, but giving them the space and time they needed to find their words.

After a few long moments, Eric said all in a rush, "Look. It probably isn't my business. But I know something's wrong. We all do. The magic isn't working."

Tara nodded slowly. Kaede had never hid that ze was a witch from zir clients. Almost all of them believed it was a pagan thing and that it was just words, not power or actual magic.

"If you need help tonight, call us," Eric said. "Not just me. All of us. We can help."

Tara wasn't completely surprised at Eric's offer. They did work as a community, and the members of the community frequently helped each other. "Thank you," Tara said, though she had no idea how she might use any of their help with what the coven needed to do that night.

"Tonight's the spring equinox," Eric continued.

That surprised Tara a little more, that the boy knew the significance of the date.

"You'll be doing magic tonight. More healing," he said. He sounded both scared as well as determined. "There's a lot here that needs fixing," he added, gesturing vaguely around the room. "I'm serious. Let us know if we can help."

Tara gave him a smile. "Thank you," she said again. "Your offer means a lot."

"No," Eric said, shaking his head. "Don't blow me off. Use us. Use our power or energy or whatever you need. Fix this."

Tara opened her mouth then closed it again. "That isn't how it normally works," she said slowly.

"This place doesn't work like normal places," Eric said with a shrug. "Believe me. I've been to other food banks and soup kitchens. The people who run those places are trying to make the world better, but they're still doing it from a higher place than the rest of us. They care, but not like Kaede and the others here. They also don't expect anything from us." He fixed her with a hard stare. "You do. You expect us to contribute. Even the poorest of the community always brings in something to share. Don't suddenly cut off that source, thinking you can fix this yourself."

Tara paused, considering. The circle had always been able to use Richard's power, as weak as that might be. He contributed something to the circle.

"Let me check with Kaede," Tara said after a moment. Maybe there was something they could do, some amount of power they could draw from the community.

Tara wasn't certain if the coven's problem lay in a lack of power or a lack of knowledge. She also didn't know if it would take more power to coordinate a large group of mundanes than they would bring in.

"Good," Eric said. He handed her a scrap of paper with

a phone number on it. "Call me. I can reach the other teens in the afterschool program. We're all prepared to drop everything and come here later tonight if you need us."

Tara reached across the table and took his hand. The skin was rough but warm, the grip firm. "Thank you," she said again.

Eric nodded, then turned and went back to his books.

Tara suddenly found tears in her eyes. She'd gotten so much better about relying on the rest of the coven instead of trying to solve every problem herself.

Seemed as though she still wasn't reaching wide enough for her solutions.

~

JUST AS THE LAST PEOPLE WERE LEAVING THE community center, a bright redhead slipped through the door. Tara looked up, surprised. "Ginny? What are you doing here?" she asked as the young hedgewitch made her way across the floor.

Ginny's coat was dark green, setting off her pale skin. It was two sizes too big for her, and she had to roll back the sleeves in order to free her hands so she could unzip it. "Here to take ye out to dinner," she said firmly. "We need to talk."

Fear spiked through Tara. "Okay," she said slowly. "I just need to finish up here." She'd already sent a text message to Kaede about Eric's offer, which the other witch appeared to be seriously considering.

Ginny rolled her eyes at Tara. "No, I'm not about to break up with ye," she said. "I love this coven. This group. It's the first time I've felt really welcomed, as a witch, ye know?"

Tara nodded, relieved. "I just have a few more things to put away," she said, indicating her little teashop. The others had already folded up the tables and put away the chairs before they'd gone for the evening.

"Can I help?" Ginny asked.

Tara silently handed Ginny the still full tea kettle, which Ginny carried back to the kitchen to empty out. Tara quickly packed up the rest of her gear onto the cart and went back into the kitchen herself.

Ginny came over and curiously fingered the black curtain Tara lifted that hid her ingredients. "Interesting," she said. "Not sure I could do that," she said after a moment.

"Sure you could," Tara said. "It's the same as making a sachet. Just...longer, I guess."

Ginny shook her head. "It's more permanent than what I make," she said after a moment. "My magic gets blown away by me winds too quickly."

Tara wasn't sure what to say about that. Then again, she was both a schooled witch as well as a hedgewitch, so she had a better handle on how to keep her magical elements separated.

"Where do you want to go?" Tara asked as she pulled on her own rain jacket.

"There's a pub I know," Ginny said with a grin. "Serves a brilliant fish and chips."

Tara kept a smile on her face. She tried to not eat a lot of fried food or grain.

"They serve big, juicy burgers as well," Ginny added after a moment. "With bacon and avocado."

"Now you're talking my language," Tara said with a grin.

They stepped outside into the rain. Tonight, their magic wasn't combining well. Maybe it was because Tara still was nervous about what the other witch had to say. Then again, the wild magic only worked about half the time. This may have been just one of those times when it wasn't working.

"Storm's coming," Ginny said as they waited for the bus.

Tara merely nodded. She felt it in her bones, the way the winds pushed at her and made her restless.

"It'll be a bad one," Ginny promised.

"Is there anything we can do to deflect it?" Tara asked. The thought had occurred to her that afternoon, that perhaps her wind, combined with Ginny's, might be able to alter the course of the storm.

Ginny shook her head. "Nope. And that's the problem, I think."

"What is?" Tara said.

"Let's get some food in us first," the other witch insisted. "Then we'll talk."

Tara nodded. She could wait. Just as she'd had the patience for Eric earlier that day, she could give Ginny the time and space she needed.

Tara just hoped that Ginny would talk with her soon. They didn't have much time.

~

THE PUB TURNED OUT TO BE ON THE RIVER. TARA hadn't realized how nervous she was of the water until they'd started walking beside it.

It pissed Tara off. She wasn't afraid of the water. It was her element. And yet, the dark rushing river filled her with a strange anxiety. Rain came down harder now. If it continued, they'd get several inches over the next few hours.

More rain than the harbor wall could handle, particularly given the broken dam upstream.

The pub was dimly lit, with neon beer signs on the walls providing most of the light. There were two long counters, one at the bar and a second that ran under the front window. The rest of the floor was filled with sturdy high top tables, more than a dozen. Flat screen TVs hung from every corner, each showing a different sport. The smell of grease lay heavy in the air.

Only a few of the tables were filled. One group in the corner suddenly cheered on the soccer players shown on the TV they'd sat beneath, making Tara grin. Despite how dim this place seemed, it felt more welcome now.

Ginny insisted on sitting at the counter that ran under the front window, so they could stare out across the gloom to the river. The front of the pub held a wide deck. When the weather was nice, Tara imagined that it would be quite lovely to spend an afternoon, drinking and watching the river.

A harried waitress came and took their order, then left them in peace. The pub did serve big juicy burgers, with sweet potato fries and apple-onion kraut. Tara licked her fingers as she finished. She was going to have to remember this place.

As soon as the waitress collected their plates, Tara felt their magic swell together. She knew that they wouldn't be bothered for the rest of the evening, though they didn't have that long before they needed to meet up with the rest of the coven at Hallowed Ground. Ginny nursed along a dark pint of porter while Tara had stuck to water.

"Ye asked me about us blowing away the storm," Ginny said after a moment. "But ye didn't understand why it wouldn't work."

Tara nodded. "True," she said.

Ginny took another sip of her porter before she replied. "Me winds are local," she said after a bit. "It's why I had to release all of me old winds back in England before I left. Couldn't have brought them with."

Tara nodded. She remembered. And she remembered that Ginny had told her that Soot was also a local wind. "So what does it mean that a wind is local?" Tara asked after a few moments of silence.

She felt a pressure to get going, to start moving, to do something. Anything.

"Yer wind won't blow other places," Ginny said. "Ye try to call Soot to ye when you're in Seattle, and yer likely to be disappointed. Don't know his range. But he's a young wind. It won't be very far. Might not even reach Clackamas."

"Winds travel farther as they age?" Tara asked, surprised. She would have thought that as a wind grew older, it wouldn't be as strong.

"Aye," Ginny said. "Some of 'em. Some of 'em just peter out." She paused, then added, "Me winds are all local and young as well. Now, if a storm was blowing up in a couple dozen years or so, we might be able to do something about it. Might not."

Tara nodded. That sounded about right—maybe the wild magic would work. Maybe it wouldn't.

"So our winds are local, just blowing around Portland," Tara said, wanting to make sure that she understood what Ginny was saying.

"Aye," Ginny said. "And yer cat is local too."

Tara blinked, surprised. She hadn't thought about it. A wind being local made sense. Not necessarily a fire.

"Ye called him with a local bonfire, one ye lit yerself," Ginny pointed out.

"I did," Tara said. "In the backyard of my house."

"It's why location is important, when yer calling a spirit," Ginny said.

"Oh!" Tara said, putting it all together. "So I wouldn't necessarily have to be in that exact backyard if I needed to release Teruko, just nearby."

"I think that's right," Ginny said.

"Why didn't you tell me this earlier?" Tara asked, feeling a little aggrieved. She might have been able to use this information before.

Ginny shrugged. "I hadn't ever thought of these things myself, ye know. I've just been doing them. First time I've been digging in, trying to figure it all out."

Tara nodded. Ginny wasn't a schooled witch. She never thought about the magic she performed. She just did it. She didn't learn lore or spells, just relied on her instincts to pull ingredients together for her sachets or soaps.

"So my wind and my fire familiars are both local," Tara said.

"And yer water spirit needs to be local too," Ginny said firmly.

"Okay," Tara said slowly. She thought she'd been

trying to call a local water spirit to her before. Hadn't she?

"I've been thinking on it," Ginny said. "Trying to figure out what went wrong that night. With ye calling the water spirit."

Tara nodded, encouraging Ginny to continue. She still hadn't figured out why the spell had gone so horribly awry, except that she knew she'd been using the wrong type of magic to draw it to her. The net had merely passed through the water spirit, who'd then turned around and used it to sink into the floor of Hallowed Ground.

"When ye were calling on that water spirit, trying to form it in that bowl of water, it wasn't local enough," Ginny said after a moment. "It was just…a water spirit."

"But wasn't that what I did with Soot and Teruko?" Tara asked. "Just called up a wind? A piece of fire?"

Ginny shook her head. "All the myths about water spirits have them in specific places. A stream. A lake. A place on a river. Ye cast yer net too wide."

"Oh," Tara said, nodding. "So even being in a park wouldn't have worked," she said after a moment.

"Probably not," Ginny said. "Not unless ye formed a mud puddle and called a spirit out of that. But it wouldn't be a strong one."

"Got it," Tara said. "So what do you suggest?"

She knew what the other witch was going to say before she even spoke the words. She still wanted to hear them out loud.

"We're gonna march right out on that pier over there," Ginny said, gesturing with her glass, "and call up the spirit of the river. Bind it to ye."

"Without the rest of the coven?" Tara asked.

"They can't help ye," Ginny insisted. "Hell, I can't either. Yer gonna have to do the calling yerself."

It felt so different than the offer Eric had made that afternoon, to help with the community center. Then again, the coven couldn't share in the power of the water spirit. It really would be a singular creature, only bound to Tara herself.

"Are you sure?" Tara asked, watching Ginny down the last of her pint and stand up.

Ginny at least had the decency to shrug. "I know ye have to do the calling. Can't tell ye if you'll succeed or fail."

The other witch's eyes suddenly bore into Tara's. "But ye better pray to Brigid and beyond that ye find yer water spirit. Nothing else is gonna save the city."

Tara grimly nodded. Ginny was right. She needed to tame the river if they were going to have a fighting chance.

CHAPTER 6

The harbor wall stands finally, and the latest spring floods have bypassed the city. I keep finding myself drawn back to it, though. I wonder if another might have served better as the wall's guardian. Eunida does her best, wandering the endless tunnels she's built there. Mulinohana pushes harder against that structure than against the bridges. I wonder what else I need to do to strength the wall. I have heard rumors that Eunida is able to haunt the ground above as well, that she calls humans to their death. I will try to set a net to trap those souls she damns, so that it isn't just a single soul who protects the wall.

Wilson Evermore, Master Magician and Hunter of Souls, 1932

THE WINDS HAD GROWN FIERCE WHILE TARA AND GINNY had eaten. They howled out of the south, warm and wild. Tara's jeans were quickly soaked. The darkness of the night settled heavily around them, the shadows hiding them even without their magic.

Just past the restaurant a private pier jutted out into the river. The water wasn't high enough to slosh over the top of it yet, but the rain had soaked it thoroughly, making it slippery. An orange streetlight bravely tried to light the path despite the heavy rains.

A locked gate stood at the foot of the pier. Wire fencing wrapped around the edges of the gate and up the pier so that someone would have to swim deep into the water in order to gain access. Neither Ginny or Tara thought anything of it. A simple touch of the hand brought the winds who slipped the tumblers into place, the door sliding open silently.

Tara took a deep breath before she set foot on the pier itself. The earth had always seemed to support her. Now, she would be floating, standing above the water, connected to the ground but not on it.

Somehow, that seemed significant to her. She thought back to being at the headwaters of the Willamette, where she'd delayed the Riprap man so they could break his bond with Mulinohana. She bet that the original ceremony had been done while standing on the boulders there.

She would have to tell Ginny about this, if the other witch ever wanted to call a water spirit to her. Then again, Ginny's element was the wind. She might never progress to other spirits.

Would Tara ever try to call an earth spirit to her? Or would this be the last spirit she had? She didn't know, but thought that at some point, an earth spirit might be kind of cool as well. She still thought fondly of the old oak who had helped her traverse the circle of earth.

Tara shook her head, the rain dripping off her hat, reminding herself to focus.

"Ye can do this!" Ginny shouted over the wind, encouraging her.

Tara took a deep breath, nodded, and walked out onto the pier.

The winds tried to push Tara into the water. She didn't bother calling Soot—he was no match for these. She did bring up that spark of fire that always lived deep within her, just a little something to chase the cold away.

She recognized her mistake as soon as she did. The wind was working with the water, who recognized its ancient enemy. Tara's next step wasn't straight but to the side as a gust nearly knocked her over.

Fine. She'd be cold. She let go of the fire, trying to appease the storm.

The winds backed off slightly, so that she was able to mostly walk a straight line to the edge of the pier. Dark water rushed before, off the edge. She couldn't see the far bank through the storm, so it felt as though she stood at the very end of the world. The rain struck her face, blowing sideways, stinging with cold. The lovely burger she'd just eaten now sat like a bloated sack in her belly, throwing her off balance without grounding her.

Why was she doing this again?

Tara suddenly felt warmth at her back, as if a ray of sunshine had miraculously broken through the clouds. When she looked over her shoulder, she saw that Ginny had followed her there to the end of the pier. Though the other witch couldn't help Tara calling her water spirit, it still made her heart glad to know that she wasn't alone.

Someone would be there to either witness her success, or to help her bear the weight of her failure.

Tara spoke her prayer out loud, though she doubted that even Ginny could hear her. She thanked not only the eastern and western winds, but those that blew north and south as well. She thanked the retreating winter spirit for its duty, teaching them the stillness of the season, the need for reflection. She welcomed the coming spring as well as the growing light, without forgetting to thank the darkness of night, keeping balance in all things.

The winds whipped her words away, casting them far and wide. She didn't know if any of them reached the river itself. It reminded her of the first time she'd tried to scatter rose petals on the water and Soot had chased each one away.

Tara had always felt comfortable in the water, had always lived near it so she could regularly see it and visit it. However, unlike the fire, she didn't feel as though she had a "spark" of the water inside of herself that she could draw from.

She blinked out across the dark river rushing under her feet. Wind drove the rain almost horizontal at this point, slamming into her. The winds howled as they whipped past her, drowning out the sound of the water at times. She shivered in the cold, fighting to stay on her feet.

She couldn't tame the storm. It was too big, too wild. Maybe if she had the full power of the coven behind her, but even then she didn't think it would work.

However, she still had to do *something*. The winds made it impossible for her to think, let alone perform magic. She still felt that itch inside to move, though she knew if she raised her arms or danced that the wind would catch at her jacket and throw her into the waters.

She felt more than heard Ginny's word, coming from behind her.

Local.

Tara drew herself up and closed her eyes for a moment. She needed to focus on what was right in front of her, the local surroundings. Not the entire storm or the full river.

Stinging rain lashed against her face. The cold had seeped into her very bones, freezing her in place. The smell of the river was very faint, but she still tried to draw it closer.

Then she called Soot to her. She thought about his slick, warm fur and clear eyes, his boundless, puppy-like enthusiasm. She couldn't free her hair from her hat, but she thought about how he liked to tug on it.

Suddenly, the winds around her lessened. She could hear again. The rain hitting the pier made a hollow sound. Ginny hummed behind her, the sound making her heart lighter.

The pressure of a warm body leaned against Tara's soaking jeans. She could barely make out the dark shape of Soot at her feet, but he was there, protecting her. His local winds rebuffed the storm, at least in the area directly around her, and hopefully Ginny as well.

Tara took a deep breath, feeling as though she'd just stepped into the eye of the storm. It still howled all around her, but she had a few moments of peace.

"Thank you," she told her familiar, her wet fingers scratching the top of Soot's rain-slicked fur.

The dog looked up at her, expectant. What else did she need?

Tara shrugged. She had no idea. She wasn't about to call Teruko out into this mess. Not that she'd come. She *hated* the water. Wouldn't stand for her fur to get all wet. Plus, Tara had no idea how the river would react to a fire spirit out on the pier. The river might decide to tear down the structure just to get at the creature.

Maybe it was time for Tara to try calling a water spirit. She'd prepared the space around her as well as she could.

It was time to try.

~

TARA SAID HER PRAYERS AGAIN. THIS TIME, SHE FELT AS if they went into the river waters. Not by casting the words out in front of her, off the edge of the pier, but by making them sink down, beneath her. The cone of calm around her went deep into the river.

Finally, she was getting somewhere. The river wasn't necessarily paying much attention to her. She still knew that she'd at least gotten some of the racing water to heed her.

Now, it was time for her to try to call up part of that water, to draw the local water spirit to her.

Tara didn't know the name of the local waters. The only water spirit she was familiar with was Mulinohana. Though his base was up at the headwaters of the Willamette, he traveled this way. His waters mingled with the rest here.

However, Tara didn't speak his name. Instead, she tried calling on the local waters. Some of the river eddied at this point, around the pier. Was it a deep enough pool for it to have its own water spirit?

At first, Tara wasn't sure if the local waters heard her or not. They were overwhelmed by the rest of the river running headlong down its course.

After another call, Tara finally found a thread of awareness at her feet. Beneath the pier sang a small, shy voice. It was a joyous song about the rain, the rushing waters, the depth of the river before it. Yet, this spirit held itself separate, bringing life to the banks here, celebrating the frogs and the birds who lived nearby.

Tara called to this local spirit of the water, tried to draw it closer to her. She praised its wisdom of staying nearby, of taking care of the creatures in its environment, of not spreading out across the entire width of the river.

Slowly, Tara coaxed the spirit up. It was such a tiny thing!

Was it not a water spirit, but maybe a water sprite?

Tara had read of such things in the lore that Richard had set her. She hadn't thought to ask about the differences with Ginny or the others.

Soot could take the shape of a large dog, until he was the size of a small horse if he felt very threatened. Teruko was the same. Though she normally was the size of a large, twenty pound cat, she, too, could stretch and lengthen out. Tara had never pushed Teruko to see her full abilities, but she imagined that the cat could, in fact, grow as large as a small car.

This water spirit—or sprite—would fit comfortably in the palm of Tara's hand, and would never grow much larger. Tara had an image of it standing like a tiny fairy in front of her, not even six inches tall. It didn't have much magic, or really much power, either.

Still, Tara was desperate. She slowly drew the water sprite up. For a few moments she actually saw it, dancing like a delicate, glowing butterfly in front of her. It cruised on the winds that Soot provided, then fluttered closer.

Tara reached out her hand. She knew they had to touch in order to become connected.

However, like all spirits, the little sprite was a contrary thing. It wouldn't come to her hand easily. It flew around her, teasing.

Then, it made the mistake of trying to fly further away. Tara had the feeling it wasn't necessarily rejecting her plea, or trying to escape. It was just playing.

Dark winds caught the tiny water sprite as soon as it left the quieter area around Tara.

"No!" Tara called. "Come back!"

The water sprite, even if it had wanted to, couldn't heed her call. The storm winds shredded its delicate winds, howling in glee. Tara heard the poor shriek of the little creature as it was tossed around.

Damn it! Tara tried to reach for the sprite, tried to snag it with her magic and draw it closer to her.

Too late. The being was ripped from her grasp. Tara watched the tiny light tumbling down stream, buffeted by the winds.

Tara stood, horrified. She had never meant to cause harm. Now, she'd deprived an area of its magical protection, what little the sprite had been able to provide.

Bowing her head, Tara grieved. She hoped the little

sprite could find its way back home after the storm had finished playing with it, that she hadn't killed it by calling it up.

A hand reached out and touched her shoulder, lending her warmth and strength. Ginny had seen what Tara had done, how she'd accidently called forth the wrong creature.

"Ye must try again," Ginny said.

Tara heard cold steel in the other woman's voice. Or maybe she couldn't actually hear it over the rushing wind, and just felt it, the knife's blade prodding her forward.

"Did I kill it?" Tara said softly.

"Eh. Maybe. Maybe not," Ginny assured her. "'Tweren't the right creature anyway. Ye can come back here and give a blessing on the place, see if ye can call it back later."

Tara nodded, sighing. She would do that.

"Ye gonna have to call the big one," Ginny said.

Tara couldn't help but gulp at the thought of that. She knew that Ginny meant Mulinohana, the water spirit that the Riprap man had been bound to.

At least that gave Tara a new thought. She'd felt as if she'd bound both Soot and Teruko to her. They had form in part because she'd given it to them.

Was that enough for the water spirit? Or was Tara going to have to give it something more? Give it part of herself?

Be as bound to the spirit as it was bound to her?

"I'll try," Tara said, nodding. She had no choice. The storm was dumping too much water into the river. When the harbor wall broke, the flooding would be epic. The angry river would see to that.

She immediately missed the warmth of Ginny's hand on her shoulder when the other witch stepped back again. The rain continued to assault her, the winds beyond her calm spot howling not only for her blood, but the blood of everyone it came in contact with. River water surged up, splashing across the top of the pier, intent on washing away everything in its path.

Tara had to tame at least one part of this storm or she'd lose a lot more than a single water sprite to the rain and winds.

She took a determined breath, and started again.

TARA RECALLED HER PRAYERS AND RECITED THEM A third time, though this time she started off thanking Bonana the water goddess for her wisdom first before calling on the other gods and goddess to aid her in her quest. When she finished, she began a hymn to the waters, thanking them for their bounty, for bringing life and light.

Though Tara felt as though all of her prayers were reaching the rushing river that still overflowed the pier, she still felt ignored. The waters were too varied between the local waters, the snow flow, as well as the pieces she felt were part of Mulinohana.

What could she do to call attention to herself? To get the waters to heed her?

Before, while preparing to walk between the circles, Tara had performed a lot of spells that used the elements, such as wind or fire. She hadn't done as many spells that required water. She understood her ignorance as well as her arrogance, now.

Still, water was her element. There had to be something she could do.

She tried calling up the water, but it was moving too fast beneath her. She couldn't control it.

Tara felt her rage increase. She would *not* be ignored. Water was her element. She drew a small pool of water up around her feet, causing it to swirl slightly, circling where she stood.

The amount of water that she could control wasn't big enough. Not in the face of the raging river.

Fine. She'd get its attention another way.

Tara deliberately called up the spark of fire that always dwelled inside of her. She reveled in the warmth for a moment, ignoring how the storm picked up around her.

It took some time for Tara to call up fire into her hands. She'd only done it before with the proper components sitting beside her, as well as three powerful sachets. She didn't have time for any of that, however. She called on the secret names of the fire gods, begging for their help as she gathered her strength together.

Eventually, Tara had a small glowing fireball crackling between her palms, perhaps six inches in diameter. She fed it her anger, causing the hissing sparks to fly up high, defying the water around them. Tara found herself sweating for the first time in forever. She raised the ball up above her head, calling again on the water to heed her, to pay attention to her call and her need.

With all her strength, Tara threw the fireball down, directly at her feet. It passed through the pier and went into the waters there. Gleefully, the fire continued to burn, fighting the dark waters surrounding it.

Tara knew the battle was hopeless. The water would eventually overwhelm her little fire.

Still, she'd finally gotten the attention of the river. The river deigned to communicate with her at last. Not in words, so much as with images and feelings. It showed her its leaping progress, how it was climbing the manmade banks. How it would spew over everything, an orgy of cleansing. How it would at first tear away everything in its path, then slow to a trickle that would seep in everywhere and be impossible to clean away.

Tara tried to calm the waters, reminding it of its other nature, how it could be life giving as well. How playfully the river could be, how much joy it brought.

For a moment, Tara thought she had a chance. The waters around her slowed and the winds lessened. The rain fell down steadily, not as angry as before.

"Mulinohana!" Tara called. "Remember your promises! The structures that have been marked as sacred to you! The lives already sacrificed!"

Tara couldn't see far beyond the edge of the pier, yet she felt a presence growing there. A dark form rose out of the water, like an inky cloud. "I remember," it boomed at Tara, sounding like boulders smashing together. "You no longer have power over me, human."

"You will heed me," Tara commanded, though she felt like an ant trying to stop a wave.

"Or what?" The river actually appeared to chuckle, to laugh at her.

Tara couldn't call up another fire. The water would also laugh at that effort too.

"Or you will be forever alone," Tara told it. "Seeking comfort and never finding. Seeking companionship but always racing away. Seeking honor but remaining nameless, with no one to sing praises to you."

"I don't need you," Mulinohana sneered.

"Need? No," Tara said. She knew she wouldn't get anywhere trying to force the water into one path or another. "Want, however? You want people to remember you. To not take you for granted. To praise your coming and the life you bring."

"They will fear me," Mulinohana boasted.

"And then they will box you in more," Tara reminded the waters. "As they already have."

A dark being suddenly loomed up above Tara. It took on the form of a huge wave, curling above her head. Or maybe a mouth, ready to swallow her whole.

"I do not fear you," Tara said calmly. "You are of me. With me. You will be a part of me."

The water paused, black drops of freezing rain dripping on her face.

"No. You will be a part of me," the river declared.

The water crashed down, sweeping Tara from her feet and into the river.

TARA DIDN'T SCREAM, THOUGH SHE WANTED TO. THAT would just give the waters the chance to drown her. Instead, she called up her air power, giving her a pocket to breathe in, at least for the moment. It wouldn't last long. Soot stayed by her side, not in dog form but as a flowing wind, circling her head.

It took some effort, but Tara crunched herself down into a ball. Flailing arms or legs were sure to get broken by rocks or trees carried in the water. As a smaller target, Tara could at least float in the water. She willed herself up, to get her head out of the water and take a deep breath.

Except…being that high in the water wasn't where she belonged. She couldn't swim, not against this current. She would freeze in a short while as well, her magical fire giving her a chance to survive, but eventually it, too, would die out.

Instead, Tara willed herself down toward the floor of the riverbank. She had to find a spot to take a stand.

The current wasn't as strong there, deep under the water. Darkness enclosed her. There was nothing to see except black waters. Though her body wanted to float up, Tara dug herself into the ground, her toes seeking the muddy soil.

Finally, Tara was able to stand. The waters rushed around her, seeking to make her bow or to carry her away. It took all her strength to stay where she was.

Despite how little Tara could see, she knew when Mulinohana had arrived, his dark shape surrounding her. The temperature of the waters dropped. Tara shivered, but kept her breathing shallow. She wouldn't give the waters the chance to drown her. Not yet.

Tara remembered the first time she'd deliberately sought the water's embrace, the warm fire fed by river rushes, the brown flames cackling contentedly, the only fire that the waters would allow. The humor of the river as she had faced it, its admiration for her audacity to come closer when she could have swam free.

Mulinohana no longer had a space for her, though. It had grown wild without any humanizing influences, because while the Riprap man wasn't exactly human, he had been at one point.

Instead, they stood in the raging waters, facing off against each other.

"You have nothing to bind me with," the waters said gleefully. "Any net you throw will pass through me. And nothing, really, to offer me."

"How did the Riprap man bind you?" Tara asked. She'd always been curious about that.

Despite being in the cold waters, Tara felt her skin blanch as a dozen souls dropped into the headwaters, fed there by the Riprap man. He'd sacrificed an entire coven, as well as his mentor, in order to take his place beside the river spirit.

"What do you have to offer?" the river asked slyly, knowing that Tara wouldn't give it any such sacrifices.

Tara pictured the rituals she'd preform at the riverside, the songs and praises. She thought about bringing the entire coven with her, so that they could help, but decided against that. The river needed her attention, and hers alone.

It wasn't enough.

River grasses sprang up all around Tara, binding her legs. She might be able to burn them away, but it would take time. She'd probably drown first. Even if she did get away, she still had to find the strength to make her way out of the water, fighting through a stream that wanted to drown her.

She was going die here, her soul enough of a sacrifice for the river.

Tara felt the dark presence of Mulinohana turn away from her. It had other business. Other humans to hurt and kill.

"No!" Tara screamed.

The river ignored her.

There had to be some way to get its attention. To bind it to her, as it were. A net wouldn't work. Nor would another fireball.

She needed something else.

Something floated past her line of vision. She blinked, peering hard.

A single rose petal undulated softly in the waters.

Tara suddenly had an idea.

Would it work?

She could only die trying.

CHAPTER 7

It turned out to be a brilliant stroke of luck, but every soul that Eunida takes now strengthens the harbor wall as well. If I could find another such creature, I'm sure I could bind it to one of the bridges. However, since I've taken Eunida, all the other beings of power have started avoiding this place, not just the travelers. It's just as well. There are too many witches still, who don't deserve such honor as protecting this fair city. Still, I take their pitiful lives and turn them into something useful. Mulinohana sings my praises for each and every soul, though He teases me by buffeting the bridges I have marked as Sacred to Him.

Wilson Evermore, Taker of Souls and Defender of
Portland, 1935

TARA RECALLED THE HYMNS SHE'D SUNG TO THE RIVER when she'd dropped rose petals into the water, both on the winter solstice as well as earlier that morning. Those petals were hers, freely sacrificed for the river.

She couldn't sing out loud, not without risking drowning. The grasses wrapped around her legs at least gave her more stability so she wasn't fighting to hard against the river and was able to stand up straighter. The cold also pressed against her and she couldn't help but shiver. Blackness like an inky abyss formed all around her.

Still, Tara strove to find those petals, remembering throwing handfuls of them out onto the river, singing praises to Mulinohana and thanking the river for its life-giving waters.

First one, then another of the petals suddenly floated in front of her. They glowed with soft red and pink light. They grew in mass, like a hunk of crimson seaweed waving slightly in the current.

Tara sent them streaming out to Mulinohana. They were his in the first place.

The rose petals found where the river spirit lurked, maybe twenty feet away from where Tara was trapped. They swirled around the dark form, outlining it.

"Come here," Tara ordered.

"No!" the river spirit raged.

The petals increased their speed, whirling now like a tornado. They made their own sharp humming noise, cutting through the sound of the rushing waters with a deep bass.

As soft as the petals might be, roses still had thorns.

They dragged Mulinohana across the space, bringing him to stand before Tara.

"I have kept my bargain with you," Tara told the reluctant water spirit. "Now, you will heed me and remember your promises as well."

The water spirit gave a heartfelt sigh. Tara had the impression that it both wanted to be bound as well as fought it at the same time.

"I claim you," Tara said, risking speaking the words out loud while still held so far under the water. "And I give myself to you as well."

A tendril of rose petals reached across the gulf between them.

Tara gulped. Was it a trick? Would the water spirit drown her anyway if she took it?

She had no choice, though. She had bound it, now she had to let it bind her.

Tara reached out her hand, her fingertips brushing against the soft petals.

The petals swirled around her arm, gaining speed.

Tara felt herself yanked forward into darkness.

WHEN TARA BLINKED HER EYES OPEN, SHE FOUND herself standing near the headwaters of the Willamette, that same place where she'd distracted the Riprap man and destroyed his bond with the water spirit. She wore a mere slip instead of her jeans, raincoat, and boots, so she knew that she wasn't there physically, but just her spirit.

In front of Tara, water rushed over the boulders in the river. Clear blue sky arched overhead. Green moss edged the bank, and pines, dark and ominous, stood across the way. Cold mud squished between Tara's toes, but she didn't feel as though she was about to slip and fall. No, the mud held her as firmly as if she stood on solid dry ground.

A contented sigh spread across the wind. Standing next to Tara, she finally saw the form of the river.

He appeared Native American to her, with long black hair braided down on either side of his face and dark eyes. Despite the age of the waters, he appeared to be in his mid-twenties. He gave her a smile that warmed her heart.

Despite his appearance, he wore western style clothing, a long-sleeved shirt hanging over dark black trousers, with a brown suede vest. His bare feet and long toes dug into the mud beside her.

"You see me," Mulinohana said, surprised, his words hissing like the river.

"I do," Tara said.

"Wilson Evermore—the being you call the Riprap man—could never see this form," Mulinohana said.

Tara nodded. She didn't know if that was because water wasn't the primary element of the Riprap man, or due to his prejudices, as he was a white man born in the 1880s and would never have seen a Native American as anything worthwhile.

Mulinohana sighed. "I cannot stop the flood," he said. "The waters are too fierce. Outside of my control."

"Thank you for letting me know," Tara said, though her heart sank. She'd hoped that just calling the water spirit would have been enough.

"I will calm the waters once they've broken through the harbor wall," Mulinohana promised. "That much I can do."

Tara knew that would help tremendously, if the waters didn't rage after the harbor wall had fallen. She didn't ask Mulinohana if he could help strengthen the harbor wall, that went against his very being.

Cool strength flowed into Tara the longer she stood there, calmness seeping into her heart. After a few more long moments, Tara finally said, "I need to get back to the pier."

"I will help you with that," Mulinohana said. He gave her a wicked smile. "But you need to visit me often."

"I will," Tara promised. She knew the words bound her soul to his, in some way.

"Then I release you," Mulinohana said. "Call on me later, when you need some unruly water brought to heed."

Tara wasn't sure what the river spirit meant by that. But she found herself in a whoosh of water, darkness descending once again.

Suddenly, Tara was standing on her own two feet again, on solid land. No, not earth. The pier. The winds pushed at her, angry that their prey had been taken from them. Tara found herself suddenly blown to the side. It took some fancy footwork to stop herself from going over the edge again.

Had she actually, physically gone into the water the first time? Or had that just been a spirit form?

She turned to ask Ginny.

The other woman was nowhere to be seen.

Had the waters taken her? Had the storm? Tara called out, using her magic to carry her voice. It wouldn't do her any good to search the immediate vicinity—if Ginny had been dragged into the river, she would have been carried far from here by the rough waters by now.

Rain continued to pour from the heavens, no longer bothering to form drops but instead, coming down in huge sheets. Tara felt waterlogged. She called up her fire spirit to warm her, but even that extra warmth wouldn't be enough to dry out her clothes anytime soon.

Tara stomped down the pier, angry at herself for having risked her friend. She nearly stumbled once, then twice, as Soot tried to get in her way.

However, before Tara spoke sharply to the dog, she looked at him.

He raised his eyes beseechingly to her.

"What is it?" Tara asked. "Do you know where Ginny is?"

She shook her head, calling herself a fool. She didn't need to find Ginny on her own. Soot could find the other witch much faster than Tara could.

"Go find Ginny. Fetch Ginny here," Tara said.

Soot continued to look up at her, his tail thumping on the wooden pier loud enough for Tara to hear it over the pounding rain.

"Good boy," Tara said belatedly. She reached out and scratched the top of his head, between his eyebrows. Soot closed his eyes in bliss.

"You were so good!" Tara said after another moment. "Thank you so much for giving me air while I was underwater, for supporting me through all of this. Good boy. Good boy."

That appeared to be what the wind needed. Soot finally gave her a doggie grin.

Tara had just taken on another familiar, an incredibly powerful water spirit. It left Soot feeling unsettled. She would have to remember to reassure Teruko as soon as she saw her.

"Thank you," Tara told Soot again. "Now, can you find Ginny for me?"

Soot turned and flowed away. His wind form maintained the head and body of a large black greyhound, but his legs were replaced by dense fog that carried the dog along quickly.

By the time Tara had unlocked the gate at the end of the pier, she heard a soft bark.

Peering through the darkness, Tara recognized Ginny's bright turquoise rain jacket rushing toward her.

"Oy! Thank all the spirits! Yer alive!" Ginny said. She raced over and hugged Tara, nearly knocking her down.

"The water took me for a ride," Tara said, hugging the other witch back. Suddenly, the rain appeared to lessen, at least where the pair of them stood.

"I was so worried for ye!" Ginny said, her tone turning scolding. "I'd been waking the river, calling to ye. Trying to give ye a place to come back up."

"Thank you," Tara said, hugging Ginny again, soaking up the warmth and bright spirit her friend gave away eagerly.

After a few moments, Ginny pulled back and looked hard at Tara. "Ye found yer water spirit, didn't ye?"

"I did," Tara said. She couldn't help but grin. "Mulinohana."

"I knew ye could," Ginny said. "So's he stopping the storm?"

Tara sighed and shook her head. "No. He has no control over the rain, or even over all the waters. All he's promised to do is to not rage over the ground if the harbor wall breaks, but he can't prevent it from breaking."

"Gotcha," Ginny said, catching Tara's hand and putting it in the crook of her arm. "Let's get to the main street over there, eh? See if we can hire us a car."

The rain beat down on them, trying to hammer them into the ground. The winds had done their job, and so had died down some. Water ran in the streets, the sewers unable to handle the onslaught. All Tara could smell was wet and cold, though her internal fire was keeping her warm. Even out on the main street, only a few cars crept along, windshield wipers knocking the water off furiously but inadequate to the task.

How many inches of water were they getting an hour? In the 1996 flood, they'd had several inches of rain in the first hours of the storm. Would they be able to save the harbor wall?

Tara had felt so good about working with Mulinohana. Though she would deny that she'd had any holes in her soul, it was almost as if he filled pieces of her that she hadn't known were missing.

Looking at the disaster waiting to happen all around her, Tara pushed away at her sense of hopelessness.

They could do this.

She just wasn't sure how.

~

IT TOOK LONGER THAN EITHER GINNY OR TARA anticipated to get back to Hallowed Ground. Buses weren't running, and most of those who drove others around had stayed home. Tara had already called ahead and let Kaede and the others know what they'd done, where they were.

Tara couldn't help but gasp when they finally reached the building. It looked as though a dark cloud loomed over the roof, pummeling the area with rain. The brick held on staunchly, but Tara knew it wouldn't last for too long. The water was determined to undermine the foundation.

For a moment, Tara caught the scent of wet rope and marsh grasses. She gulped, fear driving through her, though she didn't understand why.

They just had to fix this place. Soon.

Tara and Ginny hurried inside. Everyone else had already gathered, and they were ninety minutes late. Kaede's anger flared out at them as they entered. So did Kyle's. Richard at least seemed relieved.

And Lucius...Lucius wasn't noticing much at all. He lay flat on his back in the center of the room, as still as a statue. His mask was firmly in place, and he at least seemed human, but Tara could tell that it was a struggle for him. His skin looked as pale as his white hair, and his closed eyes seemed sunken into his face.

"So you finally decided to join us," Kaede said, zir words biting.

"We got here as soon as we could," Tara said, her own anger rising in return. "There's a huge storm out there, in case you haven't noticed."

"You said you managed to tame a water spirit," Richard said. It surprised Tara that he would try to play peacemaker. Then again, he had no magic, so he was unaware of the other energies flowing through the room.

"I did," Tara said. "Mulinohana, the water spirit of the Willamette."

"How did you manage that?" Kyle said, sounding impressed despite himself.

"It wasn't easy," Tara said.

"So you exhausted yourself adding to your collection of familiars before coming here to help us," Kaede said bitterly.

"No, not at all," Tara said, stung. "I wouldn't do that."

Except that she hadn't realized that Mulinohana would renew her strength, not when she'd started.

Kaede looked as though ze didn't believe Tara.

"Mulinohana has promised that the river won't rage if the harbor wall breaks," Tara said. "But there's too much rain. He can't stop the storm or the water from rising."

"So we still need to sacrifice a soul to the harbor wall, so it doesn't explode," Lucius said from his place on the floor. He didn't sound like himself at all, his words as cold and emotionless as the statue he was imitating.

"No," Tara said immediately. "I'm not about to sacrifice you or anyone else."

"Then how are we going to stop the harbor wall from crumbling?" Richard asked, still trying to sound reasonable to everyone.

"I have an idea," Tara said, turning to Kaede. "Did you bring everyone here?"

Kaede nodded. "I did. They're all in the kitchen."

"What are you talking about?" Lucius said. "You mean that mob of unruly teens in the other room? What can they possibly do?" At least he was starting to sound a little more like himself, being dismissive of everyone else.

"We don't have to sacrifice your soul," Tara said. "We just need to siphon off enough energy and power to protect the harbor wall. Eunida will leave. We can't, and shouldn't, prevent that. Let her soul be free. We'll have to protect the wall in another way."

"Will it work?" Kyle asked quietly.

"It has to," Tara said. "Or we'll all be lost."

KAEDE WORKED WITH ERIC AND THE OTHER TEENS FROM the community center who sat in a circle on the floor in the kitchen. Ze got them arranged, holding hands. A few adults had joined them as well, wanting to help.

Tara didn't try for a fancy pentagram again, though she knew that she'd be directing the energy. Maybe there would be times when she needed to stand apart from the rest of the coven, but not that night.

It was close to ten o'clock by the time they were ready. Tara, Ginny, and Kyle had created a few powerful sachets to protect the room they stood in, placing them in the corners. The scent of lavender and rosemary flitted through the air, as well as the smell of pine and sage. Outside, the sound of rain continued to beat down.

As they took each other's hands, the lights flickered. It didn't surprise Tara that the power was being finicky. Trees had probably already started falling, their root balls compromised by the water, then pushed over by the winds. More than one transformer had probably already been destroyed by falling tree limbs, though she hadn't heard any explosions.

Lucius had risen to his feet, but barely seemed able to stay there, swaying from one side to the other, as if he'd topple over at the slightest provocation. At least that brought a familiar grimace to his face.

A huge surge of power flowed through the circle as Tara started leading the prayers. She continued with her thanks to Brigid, though her eyes flickered over to Kaede, who nodded.

Huh. Seemed that ze was able to harness a lot of power from the mundanes sitting in the other room. Tara suspected that wasn't normally the case, but these people were part of their community. And demanded the right to help tonight.

When Tara finished thanking the gods and goddesses who looked after them, she gathered the group together in the same shape that Lucius had taken them before, that strong bubble of magic around them, as she went seeking the harbor wall.

At first, she couldn't find it. It was dark outside, all around her. She had no guiding points. At least when they'd been at the harbor wall, all Lucius had had to do was to direct them down.

She had no idea what direction to go in. Their soul form had no point to direct them. Everything felt shapeless, cold and dark.

Finally, Tara found a landmark: the river. It flowed like a lifeline across her own soul. It occurred to her that she could now be anywhere in Portland or possibly anywhere in the world and she'd always know where the river ran.

As Tara drew them closer to the river, it was easy for

her to find the wall. Its hard, straight line irritated her. It felt unnatural to her water sense. She had to bring back in her human senses, to remind herself of the good the wall would do, before she butted against it in disgust.

Diving deep under the river, she was able to find a chink in the wall, and slide the group through, into the empty space where Eunida lived.

You've come.

The words echoed around them. Cold rock walls encased them, and even colder winds blew through the tunnels. The dirt under their feet felt as powdery as ash. A ghostly light—like that from beyond the grave— emanated from all around.

And here, you'll die.

Sharp points of energy tried to pierce the protective shell that Tara maintained around the coven, like a bevy of arrows.

Most of the points bounced off the magic shield that Tara maintained. The only one that got through reached Lucius. It was like a harpoon, meant to drain out his soul into the wall around them, the point connected to a solid line, as thick as Tara's arm.

"No," Tara said. She burned the rope connecting Lucius to the harbor wall in a flash.

Tara felt more than heard the sigh as the other being turned away.

It's all on your head, then.

It surprised her that Eunida appeared to give up so easily, only sending a single volley their way. But the being was leaving.

Would she go peacefully?

A rush of energy filled the chamber they stood in, as if a spigot had just been turned on.

Damn it! Eunida was intent on destroying the prison that had held her for so long. Not that Tara blamed her for being vindictive. She might have done the same after being held against her will, imprisoned when all she wanted to do was to roam free.

Still, she had to stop the other being from destroying the harbor wall, particularly as they were reaching the critical point in the flood.

Tara tried a familiar net to sling around Eunida, to try to contain the energy surging around them. However, it was as effective as it had been for catching water.

Kyle surprised her by stepping forward. *Let me.*

It was the first time that he'd tried directing the energies of the coven. It wasn't that he wasn't comfortable with the group. He'd just never believed it to be his place.

Yet, Kyle was a fourth level witch. He'd walked to the circle of water right after Tara had met him.

Tara saw her mistake immediately. The circle of water wasn't just about the element. It was also about process. It was the ability to put plans into place, to work with the entire coven instead of focused on an individual's power.

Plus, Kyle's greatest strength lay in his ability to stay calm under fire. Though he didn't practice as a lawyer, he still got into debates regularly, and had to stay cool when regularly faced with challenges.

Kyle's power washed over Tara like a soothing balm. She hadn't realized how angry and fearful she'd been feeling. If she'd been a cat, her hackles would have been raised all along her spine, her tail bushed out.

Though she'd teased Kyle about having a great, late-night jazz, smooth voice, she hadn't ever thought about the fact that he did in fact, listen to jazz on a regular basis. The sound of a saxophone, low and sweet, floated through the air.

Eunida didn't manifest. Tara never caught a glimpse of the being's ghostly form. However, she did feel as though the creature settled down, the music calming her explosive energy, dampening down her frantic flight.

Tara and the others shored up Kyle's power, sending more his way so he could slow down Eunida's haste.

Finally, with a loud sigh, Eunida left the area, her soul freed from her prison. Tara didn't know where she would go. Had the being died? Or would she roam and haunt someplace else?

The circle all gave thanks to Kyle for diffusing the situation.

However, all this meant was that the harbor wall wouldn't explode as the waters climbed.

They still had to stop it from breaking to pieces.

Somehow.

As the group paused before starting the next phase of their battle, Lucius's power suddenly rose up. The being tried to grab at all the power of the coven, direct it toward himself.

Was Lucius about to sacrifice himself? That seemed so selfless and out of character for him.

Still, his grab had the feeling of finality to it.

"No," Tara said. She knew she'd said the word out loud, her body, left far behind, speaking it.

That appeared to startle Lucius enough that Kaede was able to take the reins of power instead.

Your loss, he appeared to say.

Tara sent a surge of reassuring thought his way. They weren't about to lose him. Not tonight.

He didn't appear to appreciate it, however, shrugging it away like a duck shedding water.

Even though this was not Hallowed Ground, Kaede was still their expert on buildings and structures. Ze understood how things were built.

And ze had the power of the community behind zir.

Kaede took all their consciousness down further, past the chambers where Eunida had spent her exile, into the very foundation of the harbor wall itself.

The concrete forms bulged here, no longer straight. Decades of pressure from the structure above, as well as being pushed at by the river, had deformed them. In addition, the concrete itself was beginning to crumble.

They couldn't save the wall, make it into a formidable structure again. That would take even more power than what they had, which was a considerable amount. Tara felt as though she rode at the top of a powerful wave, carefully surfing, always just on the edge of being engulfed and drowned.

Kaede did what she could to strengthen the foundation. She siphoned off the power of the community, using those individuals to hold up the wall instead of the coven's magic.

It surprised Tara how easily the slight energy from the teens slid into the concrete down here. It wasn't until she started paying closer attention that she realized what had happened.

Richard had reported that Eunida had sung more than one soul to its death. He couldn't prove her influence, but he believed that she'd killed people regularly through the years.

Somehow, the souls that Eunida had taken had slipped into the wall itself, helping to hold it up. They weren't enough, not on their own. But they'd reinforced the structure.

Had that been the doing of the Riprap man? Had he formed a trap, so that the people Eunida killed wouldn't go to waste?

As Kaede shored up one section at a time, weaving in the strength of the community without leaving their spirits trapped there, Tara finally saw those other souls escaping. Wisps of fog slipped out from between the cracks and crevices. The soft sound of sighs floated around her. She smelled the river strongly now, the scent of decaying reeds all around her.

Finally, Kaede drew back. The harbor wall wouldn't hold for long. The damage was too extensive. However, instead of exploding or completely disintegrating, it would slowly erode, failing over the next year instead of minutes.

Lucius appeared to recover his immense strength as they finished. He put a hard shell on the wall, giving it a little extra life, before he gently took them all back, up to their bodies waiting patiently for them in the community center.

Tara opened her eyes to darkness as she let go of the other's hands. The power had gone out. She shivered, suddenly cold.

No, it wasn't that. Something else had gone wrong. A muffled booming sound came from deep beneath her, setting the soles of her feet to tingle.

Something was attacking Hallowed Ground.

Was it Eunida? Had she given up her revenge on the harbor wall in order to attack them here?

No. It wasn't her.

It was the Riprap man, finally come for all their souls.

CHAPTER 8

Though I am bound to Mulinohana, I was originally an engineer, familiar with stone and brick. I marvel at how Portland continues to build and thrive. While I cannot protect all her buildings, I can make it easier for new ones to grow, by helping to clear out the old structures that are in the way. I still know rock and stone, and helping to tear down a rotting structure has become its own joy.

Wilson Evermore, Protector as well as Destroyer of Portland, 1935

HALLOWED GROUND CREAKED, THE OLD TIMBERS complaining, as if a great wind pushed at them. The windows rattled, shaking in their casements, shuddering at the mighty pressures being exerted. Cold bit at Tara's nose and fingers, seeking to encase her bones and make her creak as well. The smell of rotting beams rose up, as if the wood had been long submerged in dank waters.

Like the others, Tara felt exhausted. Repairing the harbor wall had taken everything she'd had. She'd been hoping that Hallowed Ground could hang on for one more day before they got around to strengthening the protection spells.

They'd run out of time.

It made sense that the Riprap man would attack now, while the building was at its most vulnerable and its defenders were drained.

Rock was his element, after all, not water.

"Form the circle again! Quickly!" Kaede commanded, reaching out to gather the others to zir.

Tara gulped down her disappointment. She just wanted to rest. Even her soul felt bruised at this point.

Reluctantly, Tara reached out lead-weighted hands to Kyle on one side of her and Richard on the other. They were both as exhausted as she was. Their sighs filled the room.

Shake it off.

Tara felt as much as heard the words. She wasn't sure where they were coming from, who'd spoken them. She tried to squelch the resentment she felt. There was a *reason* why she was so tired. It wasn't whining or complaining.

Kaede started her prayers, calling on Brigid and Sammil to defend the earth and its people.

A breeze tickled Tara's neck, distracting her and sending shivers across her shoulders. It took her a moment to realize that it was one of Ginny's winds, not Soot.

She felt the encouragement from the other

hedgewitch to call up her own familiars. Tara didn't see how they could help. Hopefully, calling them wouldn't drain her further.

The image of the black greyhound formed in Tara's mind, his fur warm and sleek under her fingers. A sudden gust raced around her, like a puppy chasing its tail, before she felt the warm pressure of a dog's body pressed against her leg. He'd grown slightly in size, and his head reached her hips.

All that happy energy from Soot welled up inside Tara. She couldn't help but smile at its bubbly nature. She did what she could to spread it out to the other witches. There wasn't a tremendous amount, and it wouldn't last, but it was a nice boost. Ginny's winds also helped, giving them one last push.

Tara knew she should be paying more attention to Kaede and the welcoming prayers. She had a job to do.

Still, she reached out to Teruko. The cat was not interested in leaving her warm bed. She didn't want to come to the cold community center. After a little coaxing, Teruko finally deigned to drape herself around Tara's neck like a living fur muff.

Tara shared Teruko's warmth with the rest of the coven. Teruko gave a rumbling purr of approval that finally, she was being appreciated.

Kaede nodded in approval as ze continued zir prayers, leading the others in a hymn of gratitude.

Tara found herself wishing Kaede would hurry up and finish so that they could get to the task at hand. Then she chided herself for her impatience: they needed to weave themselves tightly together in order to do the important work ahead of them. It wouldn't do to just rush in.

Was Mulinohana the source of some of Tara's impatience? She thought he might be. Though Tara considered herself disciplined, happy to be like water and just drip, slowly seeking her way in, another part of water was its rushing nature, how it overflowed and overwhelmed barriers.

Tara reached out to the water spirit, then was surprised to find that he already stood beside her. She would never have to call him like she did the others. He was as much a part of her as her own breath. She hadn't added him so much as become more aware of her own water nature.

Could the rest of the coven see him? Feel him? She doubted it. All they probably saw or felt was herself, extended.

Kaede finally finished her prayers and started weaving the group together. This time, though, it wasn't a net. Instead, it felt airy to Tara, as though Kaede spun them into cotton candy. However, there were sharp bits woven into the fluffy cotton. It took Tara a while to realize that what Kaede was crafting them into was more like heavy duty insulation.

What good would that do against the Riprap man?

Tara knew that he was still there, deep under the earth, gleefully ripping out the roots of Kaede's spells, infecting the space beneath them with soft sand that would cause the building to sink further, disrupting its solid foundation. Given enough time, the building would crack and fall over.

Kaede directed the consciousness of the coven downward. Tara felt the solid footprint of the building all around her. Kaede pushed out their awareness, shoring up the walls, stuffing every crack and crevice with their insulated magic.

Only after a piece was in place did Kaede harden the substance, making the walls solid again. Tara finally saw the wisdom in starting soft, as a harder substance wouldn't mold to the broken surfaces.

However, it wasn't going to be enough. They didn't have enough magic or strength.

The Riprap man was just going to come behind them and tear out everything, undo all the work they'd just done.

Kaede was fantastic at building community, bringing together a force that was greater than just the individuals combined.

They were going to have to have an actual confrontation with the Riprap man this time. Not merely act as a distraction.

Tara pulled back from the rest of the group, leaving as much of her energy with them as she could. As Lucius had done with Eunida, his spirit turned away to confront the other being, Tara turned as well, coming face to face with the Riprap man.

He looked better than the last time she'd seen him. No longer under the influence of a water spirit, he'd been able to solidify his body. He still wore pants and a bowler hat. Strangely enough, his string tie had also reappeared around his neck, black against the brown stone. His chest was bare, showing his rock torso. He no longer hunched to the side. The rocks weren't solid, one against another; they still looked like individual stones piled up. However, they were more balanced.

She could also see his face clearly, his pale blue eyes, broad forehead, and weak chin. He gave her a cruel smile, telling her just how much damage he intended to cause.

"You will leave this space," Tara commanded firmly.

The Riprap man just laughed at her as he reached down and grabbed something at his feet. As he stood, he tore out another one of Kaede's protection spells. It took the form of a great root, dangling in his hand, twitching. He didn't even deign to speak to Tara as he went searching for another spell to destroy, his eyes trained on the ground beneath him.

Tara tried to call up a spark of fire, but her spirit form didn't have that much substance to it. Instead, it just caused her to glow brighter down here in the darkness.

Besides, how could fire damage rock? Wind wouldn't do her much good down here either.

The Riprap man glared at her. Suddenly, Tara felt the press of solid earth all around her. She was trapped in the dirt.

He couldn't drown her in water, so now he tried to do so in earth.

The soil clamped down all around Tara, caging her in, stealing what little heat she had. It held her arms at her sides, intent on entombing her.

The Riprap man found another of Kaede's spells and yanked it from the earth.

Tara found her words were silenced. The earth had no need for sound. It wouldn't carry her threats or her promises.

How do you stop rock?

The comforting sound of rushing water reached Tara's ears. Mulinohana had been bound to the Riprap man for more than a century. And the water had also almost destroyed the creature, knocking the stones out of place.

Tara called forth Mulinohana. The spirit joyfully rushed forward, knocking the Riprap man from his feet.

"You!" the Riprap man thundered. "You will not turn against me. I know you."

The water ignored the Riprap man as it streamed around him, intent on pushing the rocks that formed his body apart.

The Riprap man grew dark, his stone turning from a light brown to an inky black. He roared through the earth, his hands grappling with the water pouring all around him.

Mulinohana ignored the Riprap man and continued his slow but steady work.

"You will obey me!" the Riprap man howled. "You made me!"

Mulinohana didn't pause. "And I can unmake you," the water hissed.

"You failed before," the Riprap man boasted. "You will fail again."

"He will succeed, this time," Tara said. The earth released her and she took a step closer.

The Riprap man sneered at her. "Why? Because you'll help him?"

"Yes," Tara said. She threw all her power at bolstering Mulinohana, strengthening the flow of the water.

"No!" the Riprap man called out in surprise. "Stop!"

"Why?" Tara asked. She had no doubt that she could do this. She would tear the Riprap man to pieces, shatter his stones and cast the dust to the winds.

He gulped, appearing shaken by the images he saw.

The darkness in Tara's soul held no surprise for her. She'd always known those abysmal places lurked, deep inside of her. Her destructive urges were cool and calculating, not hot and rash. She always speculated about choosing the worst path, of doing evil instead of good.

"You'll never be free of the stain," the Riprap man proclaimed. "You'll always be a dark witch if you do this."

Tara blinked at the vision the Riprap man gave her, of how much she'd seek death, how the dying of others would begin to delight her. How bored she would grow of the light, looking for the dark side in everything.

Was that how Miss Lucy saw the world? Tara wouldn't doubt it. Her former mentor had a darkness to her that no amount of sunlight would cast away.

As much as Tara might regret it, she knew she shouldn't kill the Riprap man. She'd known it before, when she and the rest of the coven had broken his bond with his water spirit, Mulinohana. If she chose to use that dark power to kill the Riprap man now, she'd never be free of that influence.

"Then leave," Tara said after a few moments. "Never threaten this place again."

The Riprap man glared at her, his fists clenched.

Was he determined to sacrifice himself? So that she would have to live with the shame of killing him?

"I will go," the Riprap man announced, as if the idea had just come to him, and not been suggested by not merely a woman, but a witch. "I will not return here. I will leave your special space alone."

The water surrounding the Riprap man lessened from a stream to a mere trickle. When it had finally diminished to merely a small puddle at his feet, with one last glare, the Riprap man disappeared.

Tara knew that wasn't the last of him. She'd have to battle him again. But finally, true healing could begin.

Without Tara asking him to do it, Mulinohana rounded up the wild water that had seeped into the building's foundations, drawing it up and out, so that Kaede's spells could take hold once again. Tara felt the rushing of the water as it left, trailing across her fingertips as though she'd just stuck them into a cool stream.

It wasn't an apology from the wild waters. Not exactly. Just acknowledging the one who'd called them forth in the first place, as well as her right to send them away.

Tara turned back to the rest of the coven. Kaede was busily shoring up the foundation with their help.

A new surge of power went through the group, bolstering their power. Tara felt as though she could suddenly take a deep breath. What was that? Was it just the ominous presence of the Riprap man, finally gone?

No. Tara had been working on drawing apart the various flavors of power of the coven, trying to identify each strand. Ginny's ran red hot, of course, as brightly lit as her hair. Richard's was the most similar to hers, though he didn't have the strength of any of the witches. At the same time, his always felt like a bass line to the music they played. Not exciting, but solid and reliable.

Lucius was all things string, frenzied and powerful, lifting them up. Kyle's, for all his smooth jazz, was still a drumbeat like a heart, solid and steady, giving them strength. Kaede's matched Kyle's the closest, though zirs was more tinkling, almost like a piano.

Tara didn't know what her own power sounded like when joined to the others. Perhaps she was the wild flute that stirred them and led them on.

But this new surge of power didn't have the feeling or sound of any of the rest of the coven.

It took Tara a moment to place the chorus that had joined them.

This was the singing of the choir, the community. Eric and the others. How had they managed to send down more power? What was helping them? It wasn't the Riprap man, Tara knew that.

The mystery wasn't solved until Kaede had finished her work among the roots of Hallowed Ground, reweaving all her protection spells, making them firmer than ever.

The coven would still have to spend time during the summer solstice to bolster them. However, the building was no longer vulnerable.

Tara opened her eyes to soft light. Candles and oil lamps surrounded them.

As did a wide variety of the homeless, as well as the adults from the community.

As Tara released Richard's and Kyle's hands, she heard the hymn the group was singing. Out of tune and dragging, but the effort made their words shine brightly. *Amazing Grace*, leading them all home.

Tara found herself in tears as she turned around. Eric stood close to her, grabbing her before her legs failed her and she collapsed onto the ground.

"Did you call them?" Tara asked, not sure if she should laugh or cry or both.

"Yes," Eric said. "You needed more than we could give."

Tara knew that Eric had no magic. He was as mundane as most of the rest of the community. Still, he'd felt the coven's need and done what he could to sustain them.

"You were right," Tara said. "Thank you."

He beamed at her. Suddenly, the lights flickered back on. Everyone gave a ragged cheer.

All the witches sat on the floor, surrounded by helpers. Even Lucius, though it was an older man who sat with him, a vet who'd been out on the street for years but had finally found his way back. He and Lucius sat silently together, brothers in arms, sharing strength.

The room felt *right* again, in ways that Tara couldn't describe. Warmth flowed through the air, not necessarily brought by the ancient radiators along the wall. The light seemed clear and bright and cast no shadows.

Suddenly, the smell of tomatoey goodness filled the room. Alaska, one of Kaede's primary volunteers, came into the room bearing mugs of soup, followed by a few others. Tara wasn't sure how they'd managed to heat it so fast, given that the power had been out. She gratefully accepted a mug, warming her fingers around it. It smelled heavenly, as though they'd added not only butter but sweet carrots to the industrial base that came out of the huge cans in back.

"Cheers," Tara said, clinking mugs with Eric.

Warmth spread all the way to Tara's fingers and toes as she sipped the soup. Quiet conversations had petered out as everyone shared their meal.

"Are we safe?" someone asked into the silence that held the group.

Tara understood the question at a base level. Was

Hallowed Ground going to be all right? Was the community still at risk of attack?

Kaede replied. "We are safe. For now."

Tara had to agree. Another battle with the Riprap man loomed. She didn't know what shape it would take. How he could come at her, her community, her city.

She did know that she couldn't take him alone.

Fortunately, she didn't have to.

TARA WOKE UP AND STRETCHED IN HER BED. THOUGH IT had been a week since her most recent battle, she was still feeling the effects. She'd run a marathon, and was only now starting to regain her strength. As she stretched, she felt her muscles pull tiredly. It no longer felt as though she'd fall over when she stood up, but instead as if she'd just worked out too hard the day before. Fortunately, she'd taken the entire week off from the Y, so she'd only had to miss a couple of days.

Today, she was going back to work. It was finally time. She'd spent the day before being restless instead of listless. She took it as a good sign that she was ready.

The rest of the coven had been in touch via text and email. They'd all been feeling the same effects. Only Lucius had gone about his normal business the next day. However, he'd been able to take care of Kyle, who'd needed it.

Ginny, like Tara, had roommates to help. Kaede had zir family as well as the community to look after her. Jeannie had been there for Richard; she hadn't left immediately, but instead had decided to stay when the news reported about how close a call it had been to the harbor wall collapsing during the flood. Some flooding had occurred—that much rain in that short of a time period was unprecedented. However, it was minor, a few homes and farms instead of half the city.

Emergency funding had been allocated to rebuilding the harbor wall over the next year. It heartened Tara to see government finally moving in the right direction, though Kaede had had a few choice words to say about the matter.

However, even zir resources weren't enough to do that work.

Tara looked out the window to her right. Bright sunlight shone in the backyard garden. She'd spent much of her time there, wrapped in a blanket and sipping hot tea, not thinking about anything, not able to do much. She'd truly enjoyed her hiatus.

But now, it was back to work.

Tara groaned when she pushed herself up to sitting. Not because her muscles ached. Or rather, not just because her body still hurt.

An envelope sat on the floor directly in front of the closed door.

Damn it! Was the Riprap man going to accuse her of yet another death?

Though Tara would never get a straight answer from Mulinohana, she knew that the river spirit had been responsible for some of the deaths over the past six months. He'd sung to the hopeless, encouraging their sacrifice.

Tara didn't quite understand, but Mulinohana had been lonely without the Riprap man. He'd tried to capture the souls that died, but hadn't been able to keep them or talk with them. Yet, he'd kept trying.

Hopefully the number of bodies fished out of the river would go down, now that both Mulinohana as well as Eunida were no longer acting as sirens.

Tara called up both Soot and Teruko as she wrapped her ratty green bathrobe around her. Mulinohana wouldn't manifest physically most of the time, but she still felt his cool presence supporting her.

After a brief moment of quiet prayers, asking for strength, Tara folded herself up and sat neatly on the floor, her legs not protesting too badly. Teruko immediately claimed her spot in Tara's lap, sitting and purring up a storm, while Soot leaned against Tara's side.

The envelope felt like all the others, plain manila, unsealed. It smelled like paper, not the river or even like sunbaked stone.

Tara slid out the paper from the envelope and unfolded it.

It wasn't a newspaper clipping. Instead, it appeared to be a grainy black and white photocopy of a topo map. Tara hadn't spent a lot of time reading topo maps, but she believed the wavy lines indicated hills or mountains. She didn't see any rivers.

What drew her eye, though, was the red circle around the what appeared to be a valley. It was in the middle of absolutely nowhere. There were no roads running in or out of the area.

The words, "I AM COMING FOR YOU" were drawn underneath the circle.

Tara peered more closely at the map. She finally made out the name of the valley that the Riprap man had circled.

Forest Green.

That name sounded familiar. Teruko protested as Tara picked her up and moved her to the side so that she could stand up and grab her phone.

Shock and horror filled Tara when she pulled up the news about the valley.

It had suffered a minor earthquake over the weekend. Not enough to damage anything, not really. Just shockwaves through the earth.

A practice earthquake.

The Riprap man was coming for them. For all of them. Everyone up and down the west coast.

He was going to make sure that The Big One finally hit.

And Tara was going to have to stop him.

I almost feel grateful that witch removed the bond I had with the water spirit Mulinohana. I had considered him a god. I can see how foolish that belief had been. There is no god, at least not down here on Earth. There are only mortals and spirits. But they shall all meet their true creator, one day. And some will meet it sooner, such as Tara and the rest. She removed the restrictive influence of the water, and has shown me where my true strength lies, in the earth. I have protected Portland for over a century. No more. Nothing binds me now.

Wilson Evermore, Destroyer of Portland and the West Coast, 2019

READ MORE!

Be sure to read all the books in The Witch's Progress
Series!

Circle of Air
Circle of Fire
Circle of Water
Circle of Earth

ABOUT THE AUTHOR

Leah Cutter writes page-turning fiction in exotic locations, such as a magical New Orleans, the ancient Orient, Hungary, the Oregon coast, rural Kentucky, Seattle, Minneapolis, and many others.

She writes literary, fantasy, mystery, science fiction, and horror fiction. Her short fiction has been published in magazines like *Alfred Hitchcock's Mystery Magazine* and *Talebones*, anthologies like Fiction River, and on the web. Her long fiction has been published both by New York publishers as well as small presses.

Find Leah's books on Knotted Road Press at (www.KnottedRoadPress.com)

Follow her blog at www.LeahCutter.com.

Reviews

It's true. Reviews help me sell more books. If you've enjoyed this story, please consider leaving a review of it on your favorite site.

Come someplace new…

Are you a traveler? Do you enjoy exploring strange new worlds, new cultures, new people?

Journey into the various lands envisioned by Leah Cutter.

Sign up for my newsletter and I'll start you on your travels with a free copy of my book, *The Island Sampler*.

I will never spam you or use your email for nefarious purposes. You can also unsubscribe at any time.

http://www.LeahCutter.com/newsletter/

ABOUT KNOTTED ROAD PRESS

Knotted Road Press fiction specializes in dynamic writing set in mysterious, exotic locations.

Knotted Road Press non-fiction publishes autobiographies, business books, cookbooks, and how-to books with unique voices.

Knotted Road Press creates DRM-free ebooks as well as high-quality print books for readers around the world.

With authors in a variety of genres including literary, poetry, mystery, fantasy, and science fiction, Knotted Road Press has something for everyone.

Knotted Road Press
www.KnottedRoadPress.com

www.ingramcontent.com/pod-product-compliance
Lightning Source LLC
Chambersburg PA
CBHW070655100726
47907CB00007B/2212